Lightning cracked, and thunder rumbled in the night.

Lexie sensed his presence and whirled, wide-eyed, to see Nikos standing in her doorway, her longings come to life. Sweat dampened his T-shirt, revealing his bronzed hardness, and razors of desire sliced her, treacherous and deep, as she imagined licking up each salty rivulet....

Dominic's nostrils flared as Lexie's scent drifted to him on the quickening wind. His gaze devoured the swell of her lace-covered breasts. He stepped forward, propelled by raw hunger too long denied. He stalked her like the predator he was. Driven by dreams of rapture. Heated to a burning pitch by the ache of trying to deny what was real. He was real. She was real. They were here, together, on this storm-tossed night. And he had to touch her or lose his mind....

Dear Reader,

Silhouette Books publishes many stars in romance fiction, but now we want to make *you* a star! Tell us in 500 words or less how Silhouette makes love come alive for you. Look inside for details of our "Silhouette Makes You A Star" contest—you could win a luxurious weekend in New York!

Reader favorite Gina Wilkins's love comes alive year after year with over sixty Harlequin and Silhouette romances to her credit. Though her first two manuscripts were rejected, she pursued her goal of becoming a writer. And she has this advice to offer to aspiring authors: "First, read everything you can, not just from the romance genre. Study pacing and characterization," Gina says. "Then, forget everything you've read and create something that is your own. Never imitate." Gina's *Bachelor Cop Finally Caught?* is available this month. When a small-town reporter is guilty of loving the police chief from afar and then tries to make a quick getaway, will the busy chief be too busy with the law to notice love?

And don't miss these great romances from Special Edition. In Sherryl Woods's *Courting the Enemy,* a widow who refused to sell her ranch to a longtime archrival has a different plan when it comes to her heart. *Tall, Dark and Difficult* is the only way to describe the handsome former test pilot hero of Patricia Coughlin's latest novel. When Marsh Bravo is reunited with his love and discovers the child he never knew, *The Marriage Agreement* by Christine Rimmer is the only solution! *Her Hand-Picked Family* by Jennifer Mikels is what the heroine discovers when her search for her long-lost sister leads to a few lessons in love. And sparks fly when her mysterious new lover turns out to be her new boss in Jean Brashear's *Millionaire in Disguise!*

Enjoy this month's lineup. And don't forget to look inside for exciting details of the "Silhouette Makes You A Star" contest.

Best,

Karen Taylor Richman,
Senior Editor

Please address questions and book requests to:
Silhouette Reader Service
U.S.: 3010 Walden Ave., P.O. Box 1325, Buffalo, NY 14269
Canadian: P.O. Box 609, Fort Erie, Ont. L2A 5X3

Millionaire in Disguise

JEAN BRASHEAR

SPECIAL EDITION™

Published by Silhouette Books

America's Publisher of Contemporary Romance

To Kathy Sobey, friend beyond compare. For countless
miles walked while helping me puzzle through this
bewildering new world, for your endless patience, your
ready laughter, for just the right measures of
encouragement, indignation and faith. You've been
midwife to a dream, and I can't thank you enough.

 SILHOUETTE BOOKS

ISBN 0-373-24416-9

MILLIONAIRE IN DISGUISE

Books by Jean Brashear

Silhouette Special Edition

The Bodyguard's Bride #1206
A Family Secret #1266
Lonesome No More #1302
Texas Royalty #1343
Millionaire in Disguise #1416

JEAN BRASHEAR

A fifth-generation Texan, Jean Brashear hopes her pioneer forebears would be proud of her own leap into a new world. A lifelong avid reader, she decided when her last child was leaving the nest to try writing a book. The venture has led her in directions she never dreamed. She would tell you that she's had her heart in her throat more than once—but she's never felt more alive.

Her leap was rewarded when she sold her first novel, and her work has received much critical acclaim, including the Reviewers' Choice Award from *Romantic Times Magazine*. Happily married to her own hero, and the proud mother of two fascinating children, Jean is grateful for the chance to share her heartfelt belief that love has the power to change the world.

Jean loves to hear from readers. Send a SASE for a reply to P.O. Box 40012, Georgetown, TX 78628 or find her on the Internet via the Harlequin/Silhouette Web site at www.eHarlequin.com.

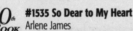

Chapter One

In the late afternoon slant of the Texas sun, she almost ran right into the sweetest '56 T-bird she'd ever seen. Lexie Grayson slammed on her brakes and swerved, muttering under her breath about the fool who would stop such a cherry car at this blind spot on a deserted country road.

A figure straightened from beneath the hood, and the scolding died in her throat.

Dark, wavy hair, slightly long. A striking face, strong and exotic features. Tall and lean, broad shoulders straining the fabric of her number-one favorite outfit on a man, a plain white T-shirt tucked into jeans so worn they belonged in someone's rag bag.

Lexie forced herself to breathe deeply instead of swallowing her tongue. "Need some help?"

His voice was deep and slightly accented. "Perhaps you would call someone for me. I need another set of hands."

"How about mine?"

Midnight-black eyes raked her from head to toe with obvious skepticism.

She resisted a sigh of aggravation and nodded her head toward her candy-apple-red '67 Chevy pickup. "I restored it myself."

One eyebrow lifted. "From what condition?"

Moving closer, she saw that his eyes, actually a brown so deep they looked black, were defined by slashing dark brows and thick lashes. His cheekbones could have been carved from stone, his skin bore a rich olive tone.

Lexie turned away from his sheer physical impact, more comfortable looking at his engine. "The body was sound—just needed paint—but everything else had to be replaced."

He grunted, not yet convinced. "How much do you know about the electrical system?"

"Stand back and I'll show you."

The faintest crinkling around his eyes gave her the first hint that he knew how to smile. There was an intensity about him; she sensed an aura almost like that of a wolf…waiting…watching. Always on guard. Power restrained by the force of a very strong will.

He frowned. "It will be dark soon. You should not be stopping to help a strange man."

He sounded like Max. Her best friend often chewed her out for impulses such as this, but Lexie had a different view of the world. It would only become a better place by putting your beliefs in action. She wasn't foolhardy, but she believed that people were basically good. And not too many criminals lectured you about being foolish.

"Do you plan something terrible?"

"No, but you cannot know that. Do as I asked and go call someone after you leave." He was used to being in charge. The tone of command was unmistakable.

She couldn't help smiling. "Max would love you."

"Who is Max?"

"My best friend and overactive conscience. He thinks I'm naive about people."

"Aren't you?"

Her father had taken care of that when he'd abandoned her and her mother when Lexie was eight. Her mother had reminded Lexie a thousand times before her death that falling too hard for a man was the road to disaster.

Her college boyfriend had finished the job when he'd pursued her until he'd gotten her virginity, then promptly married another. Lexie wasn't naive, but she stubbornly clung to certain beliefs.

"No. But I believe in giving people a chance.

And listening to my instincts.'' Which were good, except when love factored into the equation.

His frown deepened.

She took another stab, though she wasn't sure why she was bothering. ''Tell me this—did you restore this beauty by yourself?''

His proud smile was all she needed. ''Every inch. It took four years.''

She shrugged. ''There you have it. I'm perfectly safe.''

''And just how do you figure that?''

She ticked off the reasons on her fingers. ''One, you care about building, not destroying. Two, you have a boatload of patience—classic cars require that. Three, you've made a serious investment.'' She smiled. ''You're not risking anything that might put this baby in someone else's hands while you're in jail for years. God knows how they might neglect it.''

He smiled back, teeth blinding white against that olive skin. A marauder's smile, breath-stealing in its impact, but still, Lexie had a sense that it didn't appear often. There was something so...serious about him. As though he carried a heavy burden.

''The law-enforcement community would welcome your unique take on criminal profiling.''

Lexie had to laugh. ''So, are you going to let me look under the hood of that honey or not?''

''It depends. Are you going to admit that you had help with the heavy lifting?'' His gaze swept her body once more. "No offense, but you lack a certain physical strength."

"You want to see me flex my biceps. I never do that on a first date." Lexie tossed her head and slanted him a smile. "Of course I had help lifting. Brains beat brute strength any day."

"Touché," he chuckled, gesturing toward the engine with a sweep of his arm. "It has lost fire. I have already checked and there is no spark to the plugs, so I'm checking the points now."

Lexie looked in and couldn't resist a smile at the clean engine. "Need me to crank it for you?" She stifled the urge to rub her hands together. She'd always wanted to drive one of these babies.

"Please. The keys are in it."

Lexie sat in the driver's seat and turned the key with her left hand. Not even a click. She frowned.

"You've never driven a T-bird," he said. "It will not start in Park. Go to Neutral."

"Fords," she muttered.

"I heard that." He turned his head her way and grinned. "You are jealous because you're driving that behemoth."

"Behemoth—" Lexie sputtered but couldn't help grinning. "I'll have you know—"

The slashing grin was deadly, but his deep laughter did something to her insides. Lexie's heart sped up. There was nothing much more fun than talking cars with someone who felt passionate about them. Max would love this guy.

Then she realized she was staring. Dropping her gaze in confusion, she shifted into Neutral and turned the key again.

He swore softly. "It's not the points."

"Think it's the coil?" she asked.

He looked at her with increased respect. "Probably."

She shifted back into Park and stepped out of the car to peer under the hood. "I know a great parts house on this side of town. Come on—I'll take you."

He stood. So close. So big. So…gorgeous.

Stop ogling, Lexie. He's just another grease monkey.

But he'd make a good pirate. She could already visualize him, gleaming blade caught in his teeth, flowing white shirt open to his waist.

Her designer's imagination was running away with her, but the fact couldn't be disputed. The man was anything but ordinary.

"Why?" he asked.

Lexie frowned. "Why what?"

"You could simply call a tow truck for me. It would be a lot less trouble."

"Ah, but then you wouldn't owe me big and I wouldn't get to drive this baby, would I?" She smiled.

He chuckled and shook his head. "I would definitely owe you a ride."

"*Drive,* I said. I don't have girl cooties. I won't hurt your precious T-bird, I promise."

He glanced over at her pickup, then back at her, his gaze considering. "I am the only person who has ever driven this car since I bought it."

"Well, then, the car's in for a treat, isn't she?"

His dark gaze lit and he laughed again. "You are ruthless, Ms—?"

She held out her hand. "My name's Lexie."

There was a pause. Then his warm, much larger hand enveloped hers. "Nikos. You drive a hard bargain, Lexie."

"You're just trying to score points so I'll let you drive my pickup." Lexie shot him a puckish grin and turned on her heel. Over her shoulder, she quipped, "This place is only open until five on Sunday. Get a move on, Nikos."

"Yes!" Lexie jumped, thrusting her fist in the air. They shared the grin of co-conspirators as the engine rumbled to life. It had taken them almost two hours of driving and then working in the sun once they returned. They were both hot and sweaty and dirty, despite the bottled water Nikos had bought them.

She couldn't remember when she'd enjoyed an afternoon more.

He left the motor running and rose from the seat, his height, his nearness, the voltage of his smile registering on Lexie with an unconscious warming of her skin.

He reached toward her, and Lexie's heart stuttered. Slowly his thumb rubbed over her cheek and she found herself wanting to lean into his touch.

"Grease," he said, his voice husky.

As he pulled his hand away, one finger traced lazily across her lower lip. A bolt of lightning sizzled down her body. She caught her breath, only to look up into dark, dark eyes that seemed almost…lonely.

"I should go," he said slowly.

"Yeah," she answered, but she heard the same reluctance in her own voice.

"You, uh—" The dark eyes held hers. "I saw a diner about five miles back on the highway. I don't know about you, but this is thirsty work. Let me buy you dinner or a cold drink, at least."

She should say no. She had a big meeting with a new client, Poseidon Productions, day after tomorrow, about the extravaganza for a new product launch. She could go over her presentation one more time. It was a job that would take her event design business to a new level.

She frowned. She wasn't even sure that she should be finishing this job, but Max had insisted. He refused to let her forego a great opportunity when he could only suspect that Poseidon had stolen from him, not prove it.

"It's all right." His voice jerked her back. He nodded, stepping away. "I understand. You do not know me."

The lone wolf peered out from those dark eyes, just for a second, and Lexie mentally shook her head. It would only take a few minutes. An hour at most. It would distract her from her nerves over the importance of this new job. Over her dilemma about Max.

And this man looked as if he could use a friend. "I have a better idea. My hands are filthy and so are yours. My place is only a couple of miles from here. You can clean up and I'll fix us both a big glass of iced tea." Then before he could answer, she smiled. "Let me drive the T-bird to my place? You did say you owed me."

Again she sensed a man isolated from human contact and wondered at its cause. His eyes lit and a smile tugged at his lips.

Lexie held out her keys. "Race me?"

A much larger and very warm hand scooped the keys from hers. "A hot-rodder." Dark eyes danced. "The woman has a taste for danger."

She repressed the shiver dancing over her nerves and turned away, rubbing her hands in glee. "Let's see what this baby can do."

To her surprise, he followed her, opening the car door for her as though she were dressed in silk, not cutoffs. Touched by the courtly gesture, Lexie stared up at him, wondering about this man who seemed not quite part of this modern world. He looked like a pirate; she could easily imagine him striding the deck of a ship sailing the seas.

But then, everyone she knew chided Lexie for her fanciful notions. Before she could get any more fanciful, she shot him a grin. "I'll take care of this honey, I promise." Then she waved and was off like a shot.

As he followed her, the man whose family had always called him Nikos was still wondering what to think of this unusual woman. He knew that his offer of the diner was more than polite concern. It was reluctance to let her go, pure and simple. He had just spent the most pleasurable hours in many years, laughing and talking with this charming creature, feeling at ease as he hadn't in so long. He couldn't remember the last time he had enjoyed himself so much, and all they had done was swap car stories.

But he had to ask himself what he thought he was doing when they turned onto a one-lane road, then turned again a half mile later. He wasn't prone to spontaneous moves. He had so much work to do before tomorrow's early meeting, and he needed to make time for his troubled sister, Ariana, too.

He could not stay long. Should probably simply tell Lexie when they stopped that he had work to do. But then he thought about the quirky, unpredictable character driving in front of him. She didn't know who he was or how much money he had and seemed to like him, anyway. It felt wonderful. It would change, of course, when she found out. The women he encountered seldom looked past the dollar signs. He couldn't help wanting to string out this rare interlude.

But he did not have that luxury. Duty called. He would see her home, get her phone number, and then leave. It might be a while before he could indulge himself again, with his business threatened by signs of a hostile takeover. But somehow, out of his killer schedule, he would find time to ask her out on a date. He wanted more time to enjoy that effervescence, the way she reached into the darkness and spread her light. And just maybe he would get lucky. Maybe she wouldn't change, still wouldn't care once she knew who he was.

Certainly nothing else about her was predictable.

She was an odd combination of tomboy and temptress. Gamine. Beautiful. Huge green eyes filled with laughter. Short, tousled auburn hair. Lush, full lips that made a man want to drop to his knees and beg.

They rounded a corner, turned in past a mailbox and her place came into view.

Nikos hadn't been struck dumb in a long time, but this was one for the books. A dome. A geodesic dome.

Where else for a tomboy with a courtesan's mouth who got more excited over an engine than most women got over a diamond the size of an egg?

Moving down the driveway, he looked around. She had flowers everywhere, a brilliant rainbow of blossoms. In the middle of a glade off to the side, she'd set a birdbath. Hummingbird feeders dotted the trees in several spots, and a windsock flew above the dome.

He peered more closely, squinting in the last rays of the sun, trying to see the design.

A Jolly Roger. The woman was too much.

A crack of laughter worked its way out of his throat, and he realized that he'd laughed more this day than he had in a year. Then he sobered, thinking about just how much was at stake, how little business he had taking this detour. He had a company to save, and he'd only left the office to take a drive so he could think.

He should back out of her driveway right now. Head back to the office, get back on his laptop, rack his brains for an answer to the threat to his business.

But the thought sucked all the glow out of an evening made unexpectedly bright by a slender fairy with a streak of grease on her cheek.

The rap on his window jerked him out of his thoughts. He rolled down the window.

Her hands slipped into her back pockets and a wisp of uncertainty entered her gaze. "Want to look around?"

He could see that she expected him to say no. Despite her cheer, he'd seen glimpses of vulnerability every time they ventured outside car talk. That decided him.

"Is the inside as colorful as the outside?" He stepped out of the pickup.

"See for yourself." She tucked one hand in his elbow, her eyes once again sparkling with mischief, and pulled him inside. "By the way, your car needs just a little more tuning. Want me to take a stab?"

He was about to respond to her cheerful insult when she turned on the lights and speech failed him.

His eyes roamed the—room, he guessed one would call it. The dome basically comprised one big space, with areas cleverly divided by furniture arrangements. Only one section had a ceiling, the rest had just the huge circular skin of the dome, painted sky-blue and dotted with clouds. As the darkness fell, he could see tiny white lights glimmering up above.

His gaze caught on the bed, set in an alcove resembling nothing so much as a seraglio. There ought to be a harem somewhere nearby, and eunuchs to guard the doorways. A free-standing frame surrounded the bed with silk draped to form sides and a lofty, shimmering canopy. The midnight-blue draperies were caught at the footposts by deep green braided cords, and the satin coverlet bore a paisley pattern in burgundy, deep green and midnight-blue with gold accents.

The gamine mechanic had a sensual streak that befit her lush mouth. This place was seductive, almost decadent. He could easily picture her slender white limbs against dark satin sheets, and it was not a big leap to imagine himself in that bed with her. Not for the first time since they had met, his body tightened in response to her.

He cleared his throat. "Did you build it?"

"No, it was a foreclosure that I got really cheap. I guess nobody else could see its potential."

He tore his gaze away from that sultan's bed. "It is…open."

She laughed. "You have no idea how much until you try to get warm in the winter. Good thing Central Texas doesn't have much cold weather. Sixteen-foot ceilings make a lot of space to heat. The warmth all goes up to the top."

She gestured toward the only part of the dome with actual walls. "You can wash up in there. I'll use the kitchen sink."

He complied, grateful to escape and quit thinking about that bed.

He stepped inside the most sybaritic bathroom he'd ever seen and as he strode toward the sink, he could only shake his head in admiration.

A huge whirlpool tub sat in one corner. His gaze wandered over the room, the only one in the dome with a ceiling, formed by an angular span connecting the side walls to the curved wall of the dome. Someone had painted an intricate mural on the ceiling in rich blues, greens and reds with figures that seemed vaguely mythological.

A long skylight arced overhead through the mural, bringing light into a room lush with greenery and mirrors. The gleaming ivory-tile floor made a superb foil for the cobalt-blue tub, easily large enough for two.

For two. He looked at the tub and the mirrors surrounding it, imagining all the candles that lined the edge, lit and glowing. The skylight would let in the moonglow… He let his mind free to imagine Lexie reflected from every angle in the myriad mirrors, her skin luminous in the candlelight. Those enormous green eyes fastened on him, those berry-wine lips slightly parted…

Nikos swore silently and turned off the water, then dried his hands. He'd taken a drive to shake out the cobwebs, but the drive had succeeded too well. He was far too intrigued by the mysteries of this woman.

Then he glanced into the mirror and saw her behind him. Slowly he turned and crossed to the door.

For one heart-stopping instant he thought he saw the same temptation in her eyes. She went very still, her lips slightly parted. Then she gnawed lightly at that full lower lip. Nikos lowered his head, knowing he had to taste her. Now.

"Mrrowwwww—" Something brushed against his ankle. They both jumped. Quickly, Lexie stepped back from him. Nikos looked down.

A solid gray cat stared at him, blinking.

Lexie's voice wasn't quite steady as she reached down and picked up the animal. "My cat, Rosebud. She's a Russian blue. That's why she sounds so cranky—she's part Siamese, with that awful yowl they have," she prattled, turning away toward the kitchen.

"I should go," he said.

She turned back to him, holding the cat tightly to her chest, her gaze a mixture of relief and disappointment. "I haven't fixed your tea yet."

He *should* go. But he didn't want to. What did she want? Who was she, anyway? They'd talked cars nonstop for two hours, and he'd thought he'd had a bead on her without ever knowing anything personal about her.

But that was before he'd seen the sultan's bed. The colors. The lush, seductive fabrics.

That tub.

She was a mystery, a series of contradictions. Dressed as she was in ancient denim cutoffs and a skinny red-and-white-striped top, she could have passed for a teenager, a slender sylph whose short, feathered cap of auburn hair perfectly matched the trail of freckles across her delicate nose. A tomboy, he'd pegged her.

But in those eyes was both the knowledge of a woman and the nerves of a girl. He found himself wanting to dig a lot deeper, never mind the other claims on his time.

And she made him laugh. Lightened his heart, made him see a world outside his business, his sister, the unseen enemy who endangered all he'd slaved to build.

Just a glass of iced tea. That was all she offered, not knowing that her mere presence offered so much more.

"All right." He nodded. "May I help?"

She'd done more than fix tea. She'd made him a monster sandwich, then offered a big slab of pie. He'd eaten as if he hadn't had food in a week. They carried a second glass of tea outside to her screened-in back porch. Lexie fought a laugh when he saw her swinging bed, a mattress on a platform hanging from four sturdy chains hooked to the overhead beams. He was so serious, so contained, yet within him was a man who responded strongly to joy. Who needed a lot more of it in his life, she thought.

He turned, cocking an eyebrow, and smiled. "You are full of surprises."

That accent...his voice slid low, finding its way to an untouched place inside her.

She held out her hand for his glass. "Go ahead—try it."

His expression was part caution, part kid-outside-the-candy-store-window.

"Go on—a pirate like you doesn't get seasick, do you?"

Startled, he glanced back. "A pirate?"

Lexie felt a blush working its way up her chest and neck, over her cheeks. Her and her big mouth. "You, uh—I thought when I first saw you—" She didn't try to finish.

He threw back his head and laughed, the laughter rising through his strong, tanned throat.

Lacey wanted to press her mouth against that throat, wanted to slide her hands over the hard muscles beneath that soft white cotton T-shirt. Wanted to pull it from his jeans and—

Good grief. What was she thinking? She didn't do this, ever. She wouldn't know how to seduce a man if she tried. A few unsatisfactory experiences in college had convinced her of that. Her so-called fiancé had sealed it. Anyway, her father had taught her the big lesson years ago. Men could just up and leave anytime, no matter how much you loved them. So Lexie stuck to making friends of men. Only friends. It kept life simple.

But this man...nothing was simple about him. He had gone utterly still, watching her. And in those dark eyes was something that pulled at her, a devastating mixture of loneliness...and desire.

"Would you walk the plank if I ordered it?" His voice was rough. Husky.

She licked her bottom lip, then gnawed at the corner. This man devoured girls like her for breakfast. "I'd be afraid not to," she answered.

He stepped closer, his gaze intense. "I do not want you afraid of me, Lexie."

How could she be afraid when his voice turned velvety and caressing? "What is it you want, then?" She barely recognized her own voice.

He closed the gap, taking her glass from nerveless

hands and setting it and his on a small round table. "A pirate makes his way by stealing, does he not?" One hand lifted, fingers stroking her cheek, then brushing her lower lip with his thumb.

"A kiss, Lexie. I want to steal a kiss."

He didn't have to steal. She couldn't deny it to him, not if her life depended upon it. Right now, she wanted that kiss more than she wanted to breathe. It didn't seem to matter what she knew about men or what she'd done before.

This man was different. Something in him called to something in her, and she was rapidly forgetting all that she'd been sure was true. She didn't care. If he didn't kiss her, something precious would slip through her fingers. It didn't matter how she knew that.

She just knew.

As his warm hand closed gently against the side of her throat, his thumb sliding softly across her jaw, Lexie met the dark, mysterious gaze and lifted to her tiptoes, unwilling to wait.

Artlessly, she touched her lips to his, and Nikos thought he would lose it right then and there. There was an innocence in her kiss that undid him, that reached down inside his scarred soul and made him want to believe.

When she placed a slender hand over his heart, he felt her gentleness steal down his veins, warming him from head to toe.

And suddenly Nikos wanted to stand in the sunlight of this entrancing woman's joy. Wanted to reach out to her, to find out what he could do that could possibly repay her for the glow she had cast on his day.

He could almost believe in magic, standing here in Lexie's ethereal kingdom. It could not be real— *she* could not be real. Women were not like this, so free and guileless, wanting only him, not what he had.

Then Lexie whimpered and Nikos forgot all that he thought he knew. All that mattered right now was getting closer, not letting her go.

He wrapped her in his arms, slanting his mouth over hers, fighting the hunger that was growing by leaps and bounds, surging past his control. Thoughts of anything but the sweet, warm woman in his arms fled in its wake.

Lexie didn't know what was happening, what to call this firestorm sweeping through her veins. All she knew was that she'd never felt this way in her life. She had to get closer, had to breach the boundaries of skin that separated him from her. She slid her fingers down his sides, reveling in the difference between them. His chest was deep, his body hard, everything about him intense. Where she was soft and fluid, he was rock. He was shelter. Since she was eight years old and thought safety was natural, she had not felt this kind of strength in a man, never thought she would again.

Lexie twisted her fingers into the soft cotton and

pulled. She heard his muttered gasp at the same time she felt the heat of his skin, the ridges of muscle. Lexie dug in her fingers and heard him whisper.

"Open for me," he ordered. His knee slid between her thighs and lightning heat sparked through her body as his hands pressed her mound against his leg.

Desire shot through her. Lexie's knees went weak. Before she could recover, he had swept her up into his arms and laid her on the bed, which began to swing.

"Will it hold us both?" His voice was rough, low, his eyes burning dark coals.

She couldn't look away. Couldn't breathe. "Yes."

He leaned down and gave her another searing kiss, this one with very little gentleness. That was all right. Somehow, for the first time in her life, there was no gentleness in her. All she could feel was just this endless need, this heat and hunger that roared like a brushfire through her brain. Lexie pulled at his shoulders and he tumbled to the bed, his hard body covering hers.

"Tell me you want this," he growled, his hot mouth suckling at her throat. "I can stop, but please...if you do not want me, tell me now."

She wanted him. Oh, did she want him, as she'd never wanted anything before. But a little shred of sanity stilled the fingers caught in his wavy dark hair.

"Nikos," she whispered. "What is this?"

He lifted his head, his eyes dark, burning deep. "I do not know. I've never felt like this before."

"I don't—" She swallowed. "I don't *do* this. I don't know what—"

"Nor I," he admitted, pulling slightly away. "It makes no sense." She saw the loneliness returning. "I should go."

Lexie knew it was up to her now. He would stop. He would leave if she asked.

And she had a deep, unshakable sense that they would both regret it forever.

"Do you believe in magic, Nikos?" She summoned a faint smile, her heart pounding to hear his answer.

Nikos looked down at her, saw the nerves. She expected him to laugh, to walk away. Which he should.

But if he left now, something precious would slip from his grasp. It might be an illusion, probably was. But tonight, it felt real.

"I would have said no, until I saw this place. Until I met you." He smiled back. "Now I am not so sure."

She lifted one slender hand to his face, and he wanted to believe.

"One night of magic," she whispered. "It's more than most people have."

To his surprise, she didn't ask for promises. Instead she kissed him.

And then logic didn't matter anymore. All that mattered was need...and hunger...and longing for something he didn't know how to name. Something he had to have, beyond all reason, all sense, all the careful order of his world.

Her untutored caresses, her surprised delight in his touch, all of them told him that what happened in these moments would matter long after tonight. Finally, Nikos knew how he would show her what her glow meant. He would bring a lifetime of experience to the task of making love to this woman as she'd never been loved before.

He set about his task with the determination of every other venture of his life, with careful planning, with measured control—and in only moments, Lexie had swept them all away as a child clears a table of blocks.

It was new, all of it, with this woman. As if he had never made love in his life, though he had hardly been a monk. He felt curiously innocent as Lexie explored his body, stripping his heart of its world-weary grime as she stripped away his clothes. She discovered his body as though it were a Christmas present, unwrapping him with a child's abandon, free with her delight.

And she gave her body with the same abandon. As he peeled away her clothes, pausing to kiss and caress, Lexie sighed. She whimpered. She smiled and moaned. Her eyes teased and sparkled, then darkened with a desire that ran as deep as his own.

And sweet. Oh, she tasted so sweet. Like peaches left to ripen on the tree. Her breasts plumped under his touch, her nipples exquisitely responsive to his tongue. When he moved down and lifted her to his mouth, her hands tightened in his hair so hard he yelped. They laughed, and he never remembered laughing during lovemaking, not ever before. And then he didn't laugh anymore, intent upon driving her insane before he was.

Nikos looked at her, black eyes burning with passion, as if daring her to care. Lexie didn't care. She leaned forward to capture that demon lover mouth of his. She nipped his lower lip as a lioness would bite her lover when mating. Mating…primeval… basic… Lexie had never felt so much like a woman in her life. As she swirled her tongue over his lips, she felt his fingers work their magic at her center. She nearly screamed, bucking against his hand.

"So hot…so sweet," Nikos growled. "You make me crazy."

She couldn't talk for the fever that gripped her. Soaring, soaring…when he laid his mouth upon her again, she fell back on her elbows, panting slightly with the sheer rapture of the waves rolling over her. The tracing of his hot tongue into the tender petals licked at her senses like darts of flame. He teased her with light nips and long, slow swirls. The thick silk of his hair brushing the insides of her thighs in slow, unexpected moments…the touch of his hands rolling her nipples gently, then closing with urgency about her breasts—all played counterpoint to the warm satin of his mouth, pulling her to a fever pitch. When she felt his tongue dart within her, she moaned as her conscious mind disintegrated into wave after wave of dark ecstasy, electricity surging through every nerve ending, burning her alive.

She could not speak; she was barely conscious.

He rose above her, dark eyes burning, the lover of her dreams. "Lexie, I have never…" he groaned as he drew her close, placing his hands on her hips as he renewed the torment. She gasped as each new sensation slammed into her.

"No—" she pleaded. "I—I can't."

"Yes…" the pirate's smile demanded. "Oh, yes, you can. Fly with me, Lexie," he cajoled. "Fly with me."

Lexie was the best kind of lover, generous and without shame. She didn't hold back, her responses lusty and thrilled.

And then she was pulling him to her, urgent and demanding, her hands all over him, driving him beyond all control. It was all he could do to protect her before it was too late, his fingers fumbling as they hadn't since he was a teen.

He braced himself over her, seeing the rose in her cheeks, the heat in her eyes, and for a moment, Nikos wanted to freeze time because all too soon, it would be over. A curious pain invaded his heart, almost a premonition that a night such as this would never come again.

It should not surprise him. He still wasn't sure it wasn't all a dream.

"Now, Nikos," she whispered. "Take me now. Steal my soul."

If it was a dream, he would never forget it. And he would pray to dream it again, night after night.

"I think you beat me to it, sweetheart," he said, his voice rough to his own ears. Then with one deep thrust, he made them one.

Lexie gasped, and Nikos stilled, a groan working its way up from his throat. He watched her eyes widen and wondered if she could possibly feel as good as he did.

And then she smiled so rich and wicked that he thought perhaps he'd found his pirate queen. He bent to her mouth and thought no more, wanting only to go deeper, to capture the elusive temptress with grease under her fingernails and laughter in her eyes.

He growled low in his throat, and her breath caught at the feel of him filling and stretching her. He closed his eyes, pausing for a moment.

"Lexie, I—you are more than I ever—"

She placed a finger on his lips and covered his mouth with her own, hungrily. Galvanized, he began to move again. She felt his every response as if it were her own. She felt his skin hot against hers. She reeled, faint from the pleasure.

As he moved within her, another storm built, eclipsing the last one. She'd never experienced anything like this, his strength wrapping around her in safety, his desire rushing her dangerously over the edge of a waterfall, her will to resist utterly lost. The night air sang with their passion, their cries and murmurs tumbling in the air.

She was lost in him, so lost she cared not at all to be found. Whirling down into the spiral of seduction, Lexie lost all sense of her surroundings, drowning in the deep, dark mystery that was a man called Nikos. She didn't care if he was a pirate. She didn't care if she went overboard into that swirling, boiling, storm-tossed sea of bliss into which he'd pulled her. Lexie entered a realm of sheer, iridescent, shimmering magic.

A magic she'd tried all her life to create.

And finally found in this man's arms.

Cresting, she cried out, and Nikos caught her cries in a kiss. He tried to hold out to take her up once more, but she was a wild thing in his arms, her eager cries and caresses demanding that he join her. It was a battle of wills won only by his greater strength, and when she shuddered in his arms again, he gratefully surrendered, losing himself as never before.

The swinging bed creaked slightly as the cooling breeze drifted across their sweaty bodies. Lexie sighed deeply, barely able to move for the sheer contentment that spread slowly through every cell.

Golden moments of pure, liquid desire left in their

wake a bone-deep quenching of a thirst she hadn't known she suffered.

As Nikos's long, caressing fingers drifted lightly across her skin, she felt, for the first time in her life, what it was to be cherished.

She would never forget the man who taught her.

Bittersweet longing for things she couldn't have suffused her. *Maybe he's different,* her treacherous heart urged. *Maybe he won't leave.*

But she knew better. Practiced in the art of living for the moment, Lexie pushed foolish longings away.

She felt his lips against her forehead as if in benediction. She closed her eyes and drank in the scent of him, of their loving, of the night's perfume. All but wallowing in the luxury of his nearness, she wriggled closer, gratified when he pulled her to him and breathed a deep moan of contentment himself. Almost a growl...definitely male. She shivered at the sheer sensual delight of his sounds and his scent.

Heart thundering, he bundled her into his arms and held her close. Lexie stroked his hair and kissed his throat, sighing softly as she slipped into slumber, her breath soft against his chest. Nikos fought to stay awake, not wanting to find out it had all been a dream.

But Lexie's magical bed swung slowly, like a cradle, and finally sleep claimed him.

* * *

He was gone. Lexie knew it as soon as she awoke.

She might have even thought she'd dreamed him, except that her body ached in delicious new places.

Rosebud leaped up to the bed, setting it to swinging again. Lexie could recall the sway of the mattress as Nikos poised above her—

She swallowed hard and rubbed the cat's head as she stared into the rapidly lightening morning sky.

She knew nothing about him, really, not even his last name. Yet she knew everything important.

She wouldn't know where to start looking, but he at least knew where she lived. Would he come back to find the magic again?

A one-night stand, Alexandra, in this day and age. What were you thinking? She could just hear her mother's lecture. Her mother would never have understood that last night had been so much more.

Max might understand, though—or at least he'd cheer. Heaven knew he'd spent enough time trying to fix her up with dates.

Lexie shivered with exquisite memories of the night. It wasn't like her at all. She couldn't imagine doing it with anyone else. But Nikos…

He hadn't been unmoved, either. She could still see his smoldering eyes. See the flare of surprise, the split second of vulnerability when she'd known that he'd been shocked, too, by the power of their joining.

Rosebud purled a trill and butted Lexie's hand with her head.

"I know, I know. I need to get up." She wanted to lie here forever, lost in memory. She rolled toward the empty space where he had lain and caught his scent on the pillow. Tenderly, she pressed her cheek against it and breathed him in.

Tears pricked her eyes and she brushed them back impatiently. He'd be back. He'd felt it, too, hadn't he?

Reluctantly, she let go of the pillow and stepped from the bed. She picked up her clothes from the floor, glad she had no neighbors, only a valley past the screened-in porch.

As she walked through her house, she realized that he'd already destroyed her refuge. Everywhere she looked, she could now see him.

She straightened. "You made your choice, Lexie. No reason to cry." Even if she never saw him again, she'd never forget. She'd hold the night in her heart forever. He'd just set the benchmark for the rest of her life—she had to thank him for that. She might never find another man like him, but now she would know if she were settling for second best. She'd had the best holding her in his arms last night.

Head high, she walked toward the shower, detouring by the coffeepot when she saw the scrap of paper, a sheet torn from the notepad beside her phone, the letters of her name dark and scrawling.

And her foolish dreamer's heart skipped a beat while she opened it with fingers trembling faintly.

Lexie—
I wanted to stay and watch you wake up, but I made promises I must keep.
Last night was special. Like a dream.
I will see you later today. I want to hear you laugh again.

Nikos

He *had* felt it, too. "Come back, Nikos," she whispered, hugging the cat. "If it was a dream, let's dream again."

She twirled across her kitchen, scratching Rosebud's head and humming until the cat yowled to be put down.

"He's going to come back, Rosie. He takes his promises seriously." With a smile, she headed for the shower.

Chapter Two

His mother was sick and he'd flown to be with her.... He'd been in an accident and was lying near death's door.

Lexie ran through a litany of excuses why Nikos hadn't shown up. Yesterday had come and gone without a word. The possibilities ranged from terrifying to merely humiliating.

Face it, Lexie. You don't know him. And men who've said they loved you have left you before.

As Lexie walked into Poseidon Productions headquarters, she knew only one thing for sure. He hadn't appeared. Enough said.

It was probably for the best. Someday she'd feel

philosophical again, able to laugh about the turn her life had taken. Until that fateful night, she'd thought the upcoming job on the Poseidon gala the most exciting development that had happened to her in a long time. It was a superb opportunity to build A. Grayson's reputation, to prove herself in a setting more lavish than many Hollywood set designers were allowed.

She should have been thrilled.

She was.

It was understandable to be nervous.

She was that, too.

She should not want to go back home right now and wait.

But she did.

And she was pretty certain the reason had a name.

And dark, wavy hair.

And ebony eyes.

And—

Stop it, Lexie. He didn't come back. End of story.

"Ms. Grayson?"

Her head jerked up, and she remembered with a start where she was. The man in front of her would have seemed very handsome before she'd met Nikos. He was just the type many women would admire: blond, Ivy League looks, urbane polish—all the respectable traits that had never appealed to Lexie.

Her pirate put this man to shame.

"I'm Bradley Stafford, executive vice president.

I'll take you to Mr. Santorini's office in a moment.''
He held out his hand, shaking hers. ''If you'd follow
me this way, we'll take care of getting you a security
pass, since you'll be here almost daily from now
until the gala.''

She gathered her thoughts and nodded. ''That's
great. Thank you.'' Most of Lexie's contacts up to
now had been by phone, fax or e-mail. She had been
here only once, to meet with the public relations
department to make her original pitch. As Stafford
escorted her down a different hallway than the one
she'd seen before, she looked around eagerly. She
already knew that access beyond the main lobby was
strictly controlled. Electronic gaming was an in-
tensely competitive field and corporate espionage a
daily worry.

Her thoughts darkened. Could Max be wrong?
Why would this big, successful company stoop to
hacking to steal software?

Looking around, it was obvious that Dominic
Santorini was making plenty of money. How much
money was enough? Why would he need to steal
Max's brainchild?

After she'd gotten her ID, they walked toward the
inner sanctum, and Stafford stopped in front of a
very intimidating-looking gizmo set into the wall beside a door that was a solid slab of metal. Lexie
halted behind him, then realized that he was waiting
for her to try her thumbprint and badge as the tech-
nician had instructed.

She felt a ridiculous sense of accomplishment when she heard the clearance voiced and the lock clicked open. It almost felt as though she was entering the chamber where she might find the Holy Grail.

Photographs lined the walls. The light was dim enough that she couldn't see well. "Are these company mug shots?" she asked, too nervous to be quiet.

He smiled. "You might say that. These are the early days of Poseidon Productions."

She slowed and looked closer at one grouping of five men. "That's you, isn't it?" She turned back to look at him.

He laughed. "Yes, that young, idealistic fellow is me."

She was struck by the weariness in his tone, but decided she didn't know him well enough to ask him about it. She turned back to the picture—

Her breath froze in her chest.

Her heart thudded once. Hard.

She couldn't face him as she asked her question. "Who are these other men?"

"Well, that's Rob Johnson on the left, and Matt Hendricks next to him. Sitting down is Henry La-Fleur, and of course, there I am."

She could barely get the words past her throat for the dread locking it tight. "And the man in the center?"

"That's Dominic Santorini. You'll meet him in just a minute."

She'd met him already, she wanted to say. From deep inside her, a keening moan wanted to break free. She knew that black, curly hair. Those ebony eyes. That same flashing pirate's smile.

Intimately.

She'd made love with a man who didn't exist. Her Nikos was a lie—and now it made sense that he hadn't come back. Her Nikos was no grease monkey; he was rich as Midas.

And if Max was right about his software—

Her Nikos was also a thief.

Dominic Santorini rubbed the bridge of his nose as his sleep-deprived eyes stared at the computer screen. The couple of hours sleep he'd grabbed on the couch in his office last night hadn't taken the edge off his exhaustion. The trading day had just ended on the Tokyo exchange. There was no question about it now—Poseidon's stock was being quietly bought up by someone, bit by bit, from one exchange to another.

His gut told him that Peter Kassaros was behind it. The man had almost broken Ariana before she had gotten away. Boyhood competitor then business rival, Kassaros had gone too far when he'd seduced Dominic's naive, much younger sister. He'd made it personal, and Dominic had taken steps to avenge her, buying up some of Kassaros's loans.

Kassaros had found a new avenue to strike back. If only Dominic could prove it.

"Dominic?"

He lifted his gaze to find his best friend and second-in-command, Bradley Stafford, studying him from the doorway.

"She's here."

Dominic frowned. "Who?"

"The designer for the gala. You wanted to look over the final plans."

Oh, hell. Dominic had forgotten about A. Grayson. He had trusted the public relations department and only had to okay the concept of the gala, but last week he had decided that the launch was too critical to not look over the plans himself before the work began on the grounds of his home. Why he had ever agreed to doing it there—

Dominic scrubbed his face with his hands. The launch of Legend Quest meant everything to this company's survival. Too many people depended on him to find an answer.

The man who'd been Nikos for one magical night remembered a note...and a promise. With regret lodged in his chest like a boulder, he admitted that he had been kidding himself to think he could afford the luxury of Lexie's joy right now...when so much else was at stake.

"All right," he sighed. "Show her in."

He glanced back at the report he'd been reading,

wishing he had a few more minutes. He heard the door open again.

He looked up.

And forgot to breathe.

Nothing could have prepared him for the sight of the woman who had been on his mind for two days.

A fierce flare of joy shot through him, even as he tried to figure out why she was here. He rose without thinking, his mind grasping to make some sense.

Lexie here—in his office. How had she found him? Damn—the timing was all wrong, but he wanted to see her, talk to her. He'd have to get Bradley to cancel the meeting with—

A. Grayson. The designer. The creative—

A for Alexandra?

My God. Under his nose all the time.

Lexie. He almost said it out loud, started to smile until he got a look at her eyes, dark and anguished. Then they turned almost…empty.

He frowned. He needed to explain why he hadn't come back—

"Dominic Santorini, this is Alexandra Grayson, our designer." Bradley's voice sounded as if it were a thousand miles away.

Lexie, you're here. Lexie, I wanted— The words hovered at the edge of his normal reserve.

But this woman wasn't Lexie. A stranger stood stiffly, the short skirt of her red suit revealing legs he could still feel wrapped around his waist—

But every line of her body said, "Hands off."

Something was very wrong, but it wasn't a discussion to have right here. What a damnable complication to an already difficult situation. With years of practice, Dominic buried his thoughts behind a granite mask and put out his hand. "Pleased to meet you, Ms. Grayson."

Still reeling from the discovery, Lexie blinked in shock. He wasn't going to admit that they'd met. It shouldn't surprise her. Others had found her easy to leave.

A dull ache hollowed out her chest. The man called Nikos had been merely a figment of her imagination. This man was cold as stone. Dominic Santorini must be laughing up his sleeve. Everyone in Austin—shoot, half the country—knew who he was.

Everyone but a fool like Lexie, the woman who seldom read a newspaper or watched TV. Who, despite her protests, had turned out to be naive, after all.

She wanted to turn around and run as hard as she could, back to safety, back to home. But he was already there, like the air, touching every part of her refuge. She had to make her stand here. She couldn't let this defeat her. It was simply an embarrassment, she told herself. She couldn't dwell on it.

She needed the job. Now, more than ever, she needed to help Max, her true friend.

Summoning up every ounce of strength within her, she took his offered hand, only to be jolted to her toes by the lightning bolt of his touch. For one flicker, his ebony eyes glowed hot with memory. She couldn't help the brief tightening of her hand on his. She felt the warmth of his skin and remembered how that hand had felt on her body in the heat of—

No. She jerked her hand away. This man in his expensive charcoal Italian suit was not Nikos. Nikos was a lie. She had to remember that.

Somehow she found her voice. "Thank you, Mr. Santorini."

"Please...call me Dominic."

No, call me Nikos, he wanted to demand. *Call me Nikos as I drag you beneath me and sheathe myself in your warm velvet body. Moan my name as I suckle your very sensitive nipples. Scream as I make love to you with my mouth.*

Damn it, she felt it, too. She had to. They had to talk. He had to dig Lexie out from under this stranger. "Bradley, would you please excuse us?"

Lexie's legs turned to spaghetti. He was staring at her like a predator contemplating a meal.

Before he could unnerve her completely, she turned away. "I'd like Mr. Stafford to look at these, too, if you don't mind." With unsteady hands, she began to spread her drawings out on the large table beside her.

Dominic wanted to jerk her around and demand answers.

Who was he kidding? He wanted to strip her naked and take her right where she stood. With a ferocity he hadn't felt in years, he wanted to get beneath that trim suit to the body his hands itched to touch. He wanted to muss that hair and smear her lipstick with his kisses. Wanted to heat that damned cool voice and shatter the distance she'd placed between them. Wanted, more than anything, to laugh with her again—but the laughing tomboy had vanished.

When he hung back, Bradley looked at him oddly.

What had changed? Was she only hurt that he hadn't returned or had he been that wrong about her? Dominic swore silently every ripe curse he could remember. Gritting his teeth so hard his jaw ached, he nodded curtly at his aide. "Let's see what you have."

His secretary spoke from the doorway. "Mr. Santorini, there's a conference call on one from Seattle. Do you want to take it?"

Lexie glanced at him quickly, and he wanted to order her to stay right where she was until he could clear the place out. Get rid of every damned person here. Lock the doors behind them and find his way back to the magic.

But people depended on him—many people. This call was earlier than expected, but it was absolutely crucial to Poseidon.

Bradley knew its importance. He spoke up. "It's all right. We'll move to my office. I'll give you a report later."

Dominic shot a quick look at Lexie, fiercely willing her to look at him.

But when she did, she was not Lexie. The tomboy with grease on her cheek had vanished. In her place stood a stranger whose posture screamed how much she wanted away from him.

Had he only imagined that magical Lexie?

It wouldn't be his first experience with masks and betrayal. Obviously what he had felt that night had been a one-way experience.

Just as well. He had a company to save.

"Fine. Ask them to hold a minute, Mrs. Murray. I will be right there." He started to offer his hand, but the stranger who looked just like Lexie had already gathered up her drawings and was halfway to the door.

Lexie couldn't remember how she got out of the building and into her pickup. Her mind seethed and boiled, thoughts tumbling over one another in horror and confusion.

She didn't want to think about what she'd just learned.

She wanted to take back the last—how long had she been driving around? However long it had been, she wanted an hour before that.

Back to the time when she could only think of Nikos as a man who broke a promise to come back.

She fought the urge to drop her head to the steering wheel and weep. How could she reconcile the man who caressed her body so tenderly, who elicited depths of passion from her that she'd never dreamed existed—how could she reconcile her pirate lover with the man who'd built that megalith of a company?

And how could she even begin to see him as a man who would steal Max's dreams?

He couldn't have…could he?

She should just ask him, flat-out—but how did you ask a question like that? *Did you steal my friend's creation?*

She wasn't even sure she could have asked such a question of the man she'd known as Nikos. But this man? This remote, forbidding stranger who hadn't even acknowledged they'd met? This man who was almost as rich as Croesus and gaining daily?

History taught that successes as big as Poseidon took intense concentration and ruthlessness to build. Where was there room for the man who'd taken her breath away, inside the man who could build all of that?

"Dear God…" she whispered. What did she do? She pulled into her driveway and dropped her head back against the seat, feeling sick. How could she have let him touch her? How could she have been so blind?

To think that she'd cried over him, shed tears that he hadn't shown up. Told him so blithely all the reasons she was sure she could trust him.

She'd been such easy pickings.

The old lesson reared its nasty little head.

Never let a man sweep you off your feet. Her mother's voice rang out, clear as a bell. *Look at what happened to me.*

She'd been more right than she'd known when she'd compared him to a pirate. Pirates plundered, they didn't trouble with something as inane as a conscience. She'd made it easy for him.

So easy. *Too easy, Lexie.*

He hadn't felt the magic—only she had.

But the note... He'd called it special, their night.

Lexie laughed, but it rang hollow and hurt her chest. He'd come back to his real life and realized his mistake. It wasn't as though he was the first to find her wanting. And he was rich, filthy rich. Moved in a jet-set crowd. Knew women all over the world more sophisticated and glamorous than she'd ever be.

How could she work with him? The gala was to be held at his house and from here on, though she had other jobs, it would be her main focus.

His house? His *mansion.* He lived in another world. *Just another grease monkey, right, Lexie?*

She couldn't do it. She couldn't work on this contract, now that she knew. She couldn't bear to face him.

Not the way she'd lost her mind in his arms. She couldn't.

Max, she reminded herself. She might be needed

to help Max prove the theft. He was her best friend and she couldn't let him down.

She wasn't a coward. She had to find some way to close herself up tight and go through with this contract. How, she didn't know, but she had no choice. And while she was at it, she had to wipe away every memory of a night that was burned into her brain. She could do it; she had practice. After all, if she knew anything, she knew about letting go of girlish dreams.

Wiping at her wet cheeks with the edge of one palm, Lexie opened the door and got out of the pickup, straightening her shoulders as she walked to her door.

She wouldn't be a fool again. She would stay out of Santorini's path, get the job done, get on with her life.

The red light on her answering machine was blinking. Weary to the bone, she reached over and punched the play button.

A strange woman's crisp voice spoke. "Ms. Grayson, this is Evelyn Murray, Dominic Santorini's secretary. Mr. Santorini wishes you to meet with him tomorrow at his home at 2:00 p.m. to discuss your plans for erecting the sets for the gala. If two o'clock is not suitable, please call me at your earliest convenience to discuss an alternate time."

Meet with him. At his home. Alone. Her earlier resolve wavered. Shivered like aspen leaves in the chill mountain wind. When would be a good time?

Lexie sank into a chair, rubbing the heel of her hand over her breastbone to soothe away the ache and confusion at the very thought of being alone with Dominic Santorini.

How about never, Mrs. Murray?

Chapter Three

"You look whipped. What's up?" Bradley asked later that day.

Dominic shrugged. "The usual." Taking in a deep breath, he nodded at the computer screen. "Have you seen it?"

"Yeah." Bradley began to pace. "You were right. Somebody's making a move on our stock. Still in little bits and pieces, but the signs are all there. And with our ready cash short—" He exhaled sharply. "The timing stinks."

"We could dip into reserves. We have the money."

"But then the stock will drop."

"Not for a little while. Not until the next report." Dominic swore softly. "If only Legend Quest was ready to roll today." The new game they were about to launch would solve all their cash problems. Its cutting-edge graphics would bring their competitors to their knees.

"Maybe we should cancel plans for the gala. That's a chunk of change we don't have to spend."

Dominic shook his head. "No. We need this to debut with a splash now more than ever." He wanted some good news for a change. Something to make him forget how badly he wanted to be back in that geodesic dome that seemed light-years away. "Tell me how the final tests are going."

"That's one thing that couldn't be better. We'll be ready to ship on schedule. The new graphics will have everyone's tongues hanging out." Bradley smiled. "Legend is going to leave the whole industry eating our dust."

Dominic frowned, contemplating. "I wish we could launch now." He swore ripely. "I should not have tied up so much of my own money in this project. I could have bought more stock and protected us."

Bradley's face went sober. "As long as word doesn't get out prematurely, we'll be all right."

Dominic sat up straighter, the cold gleam of determination on his mind. "Peter Kassaros will never get control. Poseidon is mine. It will remain mine." He looked up. "Ours," he corrected. He wished

they'd never gone public. "Since Ariana and I together own fifty-one percent and you have ten percent more, we will be all right."

"We don't know that it's Kassaros," Bradley
pointed out.

"I feel it—" Dominic tapped his chest. "In here.
I know it is him."

"Look, Dominic, I know you never wanted to
trade stock publicly. That was my idea, a way to get
the capital to expand back then." He lowered his
chin, looking down at the floor. He sighed, then
raised his gaze to meet Dominic's. "I shouldn't
have badgered you into it. We're vulnerable until
Legend Quest starts paying off."

"It's done." Dominic waved the statement away.
"We will deal with it. It's hardly the first rough spot
we have survived." He'd built Poseidon from nothing. Hard work and nerve-racking tension were
nothing new to him.

"Things have been pretty intense around here."
His friend paused for a minute. "You look tired.
Head home, why don't you?"

Though he craved the oblivion of sleep, Dominic
shook his head. "Not yet. Too much to do."

Much later, Dominic turned into the long driveway to his hilltop mansion, suddenly struck by the
comparison. His place was huge, luxurious. Worth
a fortune and guarded by a high iron fence and an
elaborate security system.

It looked like a prison. He'd thought this place important once. Now it only seemed sterile.

He wanted to drive straight back to Lexie's dome, to watch the clouds on the ceiling, to swing on her porch.

To try out the sultan's bed. And the tub.

He wanted to hear Lexie laugh, wanted to bury himself in her body again. The memories had drifted through his brain every hour since he'd left her.

But that Lexie was gone, if she ever existed. The real Lexie was no different than any other woman, after all. Able to change masks with ease.

It would be awkward, working with her on the gala. There was not time to replace her—the date was too close. And she did wonderful work, he had to admit. When he had looked at the drawings after she'd left, he'd seen the same color and imagination he'd seen in her home.

No, she could not be replaced, even if there was time. What she had designed was exactly what they would need to launch Legend in an unforgettable manner. That had to be his only concern now, not some night he had taken for more than it was.

Cursing himself sharply, he entered his house.

"Señor Dominic," greeted his housekeeper. Then she frowned. "You have not eaten. You are working too hard. Sit down right now and I will feed you."

Dominic had to smile. Mrs. Garcia clucked over him like a mother hen. She'd been in heaven when he'd brought Ariana home two weeks ago to become her newest chick. "Do I have time for a shower?"

"Of course. But hurry now—I can see you growing thinner by the moment."

He chuckled. "Where's Ariana?"

"Out by the pool." Worry crossed her forehead. "It has been one of her bad days."

Guilt assailed him. He should have been there when her selfish, grasping mother had died, leaving her penniless. She'd been easy pickings for Peter Kassaros, feeling that she had nowhere else to turn. Kassaros had seduced her, then his obsession had turned her into a virtual prisoner. Ariana had finally escaped with the help of a sympathetic maid and contacted Dominic, but she was a shadow of the fearless girl he'd once known.

"I'll stop to see her first."

When he opened the door, Ariana looked up, then rose to greet him. Willowy and tall, fragile as an orchid, she glided across the deck in a long white sundress that accented her heartbreaking beauty. Her eyes were as dark as his, her hair as black but straight and long.

"You look tired," she said.

He smiled and kissed her forehead. "I'm fine." For a moment he wished he could tell her about Lexie, but she could not help. No one could. He had made a mistake, that was all. The guileless tomboy was only a pose. "How are you? Did you rest today?"

Her lips puckered in distaste. "Nikos, I can't just lie around your house for months."

The name danced across his hearing in a way it never had. He wanted to hear Lexie moan it again. With effort, he shoved thoughts of her to the back of his mind. "You have been through a difficult time. You are allowed some time to mend."

He couldn't bear the sorrow that robbed her of hope. He changed the subject. "Bradley sends his best."

A faint smile crossed her lips. "He called me. He wants to take me to dinner."

"Good."

"I don't know if it is." She glanced up, her gaze troubled. "I don't trust my judgment anymore."

"You can trust Bradley. He won't hurt you. I'd trust him with my life."

Then, for just a second, the old, irrepressible Ariana twinkled in her gaze. "But would you let him drive your T-bird?"

Dominic chuckled. "My life, but not my T-bird." And just that quickly, tousled auburn hair and mischievous green eyes leaped into his mind again.

He had to stop thinking of her. That Lexie did not exist.

"Come on," he urged, needing the change in subject. "Mrs. Garcia wants to feed us."

Ariana smiled faintly. "Heaven knows we might as well obey. It didn't take me long to learn that even my big-shot brother does exactly as Mrs. Garcia says.''

Dominic chuckled, leading her inside. And tried not to look out across the violet hills and wonder what Lexie was looking at tonight.

The next afternoon, Lexie stared around her as she drove through the gate and up the winding, tree-lined road toward the most whispered-about mansion in Austin, Texas. The land through which she passed had been left in its native state, live oaks and cedars screening the house from those passing along the road below.

Her stomach jittered as if she'd swallowed jumping beans. *Nonsense, Lexie. It's a job, like any other.*

She needed to treat it that way, but oh, that was easier said than done. Absently she chewed on a thumbnail.

Then she broke through the dense tree cover.

There it was. The home of one of the richest men in America, grounds exquisitely landscaped around a solid white-stone structure that could have perched on a sunwashed hilltop in his homeland of Greece. It looked as if it could survive for centuries, solid as a rock, softened only by the wide terraces that spilled down like stone skirts, open to the view from glistening walls of windows, each shaded from the blistering Texas sun.

It was beautiful and cold and heartless. Just like the man who'd ordered her to meet him here.

Nothing at all like the man her prodigious imagination had conjured up on one magic-filled night. That man could not live in this merciless beauty.

She was early, on purpose. She wanted to walk the grounds where the gala would be held while she could still think straight, devoid of the confusion that had rendered her all but mute yesterday in Santorini's office.

When she'd been buzzed through the gate, she'd asked the man on duty if Santorini were here and breathed a deep sigh of gratitude that she'd arrived first.

Lexie squared her shoulders, grabbed her portfolio and emerged from her pickup, striding toward the open meadow that she had signed a contract to turn into magic two weeks from now.

She'd been measuring and marking, feeling like a vandal with her can of spray paint to mark the rough edges of the layout for the crew that would show up next. But the work soothed her, engaged her mind in the one place she felt sure of herself— her work.

So engrossed was she that the flash of white in the corner of her vision jerked her up straight, heart pounding.

A woman watched her silently from the edge of the nearest terrace. Lexie's first impression was of a doe ready to flee into the forest.

So Lexie smiled to reassure her. "Hello."

The answering smile was very white and fleeting in a face that could stop traffic.

"I'm Lexie Grayson, the designer for the launch gala," she said, holding out her hand.

She could tell they were related even before the woman spoke. "I'm Ariana Santorini, Nikos—Dominic's sister." The hand that clasped Lexie's was slender, fragile despite Ariana's height, and a little uncertain, just like her eyes.

A wounded bird, afraid to fly, was Lexie's first impression. Beautiful, startlingly so, the female counterpart to her brother's stunning looks. Long black hair gently swishing over her shoulders and the same ebony eyes.

But not the same at all. Where Dominic's eyes held power and strength, this woman's eyes were pools of devastation.

Nothing could have warmed Lexie more quickly.

"Nikos called and asked me to tell you that he's been delayed and to make you comfortable. Would you care for something cold to drink?"

Hearing that name said with such affection sent a jolt of sadness through Lexie's heart for what she'd had—and lost—on a night she couldn't seem to make herself forget.

She reached into the huge bag she carried to jobs and pulled out the bottled water. "I'm fine, thank you. I never know what the conditions might be on a new job, so I try to come prepared."

"Ah. Perhaps, then, I should leave you to your

work.'' But the lovely, haunted face spoke a different message.

Lexie's nerves were strained to the limit, dreading her meeting with Santorini. She'd welcome any distraction. ''Please—I'd be glad of the company if you'd like to stay.'' She gestured toward her portfolio. ''Would you like to see my sketches of the design?''

Dark eyes lit with the first flare of life Lexie had seen. What had happened to her? Was it Santorini's fault that his sister looked so defeated?

Could the man she'd known for one night destroy a woman's soul?

No. Lexie would never believe that.

But the cold man who ran Poseidon?

She honestly didn't know.

''I know you're busy. Perhaps I should go.'' Her voice, like her brother's, revealed English as a second language, but Ariana's usage seemed less formal. She turned to go.

Lexie put out a hand to stop her, and Ariana recoiled from her touch. Though she pulled away instantly, the reaction only increased Lexie's confusion. ''I'm sorry.''

''The fault is mine. I—'' Ariana's eyes turned very sad. ''I must stop jumping at every shadow.''

''I don't want to pry, but are you all right here? Do you need help?''

Ariana looked startled, then honestly confused. ''I am safe here. Nikos takes good—'' The confusion seemed to clear. Rusty laughter bubbled up. "You thought Nikos would harm—" She laughed again, then just as suddenly, tears overflowed.

Instantly, Lexie moved to comfort her, grasping Ariana's hand and patting her back, wishing she understood.

Ariana dropped her head into her hands. "I'm sorry," she whispered. "I can't seem—"

Lexie pulled her close and began to rock the woman, murmuring to her as one would to soothe a child.

A harsh voice cut through the moment, startling them both.

"What have you done to my sister?" Dominic Santorini stood in front of them, his face thunderous.

Lexie stepped back from the hostility shimmering in the air around them.

Before she could speak, Ariana did, moving closer to her brother. "She did nothing wrong, Nikos. Don't blame her."

"What happened?" His voice was gentle as he spoke to his sister, pulling her under the shelter of his arm. "You should be resting." He shot Lexie a glare as if somehow she were at fault.

Lexie saw a spark of independence flare, then fizzle. "I'm not an invalid." Ariana pulled away, stepped toward Lexie. "I would like to see your drawings, if I still may."

Dominic spoke up. "Perhaps another time. I must return to the office in a few minutes, but we must go over some business details first. If you'd excuse us, please?''

Ariana nodded and turned to go.

Lexie wanted to race after her, partly to defend Ariana, partly to avoid the angry man towering over her.

Ariana cast one glance back. "It's not her fault, Nikos."

"Go to Mrs. Garcia," he said gently. "I'll be inside in a few minutes to see you."

Lexie knew it wasn't her business, but she couldn't help being concerned. "What happened to her?"

Dominic turned from watching his fragile sister's back. His eyes were hard and cold. "It is not your concern."

Lexie felt as if she'd been slapped. She stilled herself into careful politeness. "But it is yours. We can meet another day if you'd like to see to her now."

He shook off the suggestion. "I do not always have the luxury of doing what I would like." For a moment his gaze intensified on hers, as if his words had another meaning.

The air around them thickened, ripe with challenge, bursting with memory. Lexie lost her footing, her sense of time and place. She wanted to lean closer, to peer inside those dark eyes to look for the man she'd thought she'd known on one star-crossed night.

Then he snapped his gaze away, and it was like free-falling off a cliff.

"These markings are for what purpose?" His voice carried not one trace of emotion. Strictly business.

Lexie struggled to pull back, to find solid ground, to recover her senses. Had she lost her mind? Had her active imagination played her false?

This is not Nikos, Lexie. She forced herself to concentrate on the man who stood in front of her, the man who'd built an empire, not the man who'd brushed grease from her cheek.

Her gaze glanced down quickly at his hand, and her heart broke a little. He had beautiful hands, so strong, so capable of tenderness, of passion—

"Ms. Grayson—"

Lexie's head snapped up. What had he asked? She was dizzy from the whiplash of her emotions.

The markings. Yes. She cleared her throat. "My crew will shoot the grade and determine the best place to set the walls of the castle, but I'm marking the approximate location that suits the aesthetics, keeping in mind the view, proximity to parking, that sort of thing."

"Parking?" One raven eyebrow lifted, and she wanted to brush it with her fingertip, no matter how much this man lacked any resemblance to the man who'd held her in his arms. "There will be no cars allowed."

"For the buses and the…the catering trucks," she

stammered. *Pull it together, Lexie. You need this job.*

And Max. Max needed her help.

She stood straighter, looked away from him and at her markings on the ground. Very deliberately, she walked and spoke. "Setting the entrance arch here will give the guests an impressive view as they come up the driveway, increase their sense of drama and anticipation." Warming to her subject, she continued. "There will be torches here, on either side, and we'll have actors clustered at the gate. We'll throw lighting up the walls to create intense shadows and increase the sense of impending doom, just as a player would feel were he really Carlon approaching Lord Vadoun's castle."

"You know the game." Dominic didn't try to hide his amazement that she'd gone to the trouble to understand more than the brief synopsis she'd been given.

He shouldn't have been. He'd seen her drawings and known already that she took her work seriously and, despite appearing to be barely past her teens, was thoroughly professional.

She looked offended. "Of course. How could I design properly without really understanding?"

"You're hardly our target audience, Ms. Grayson. One could understand if you lacked enthusiasm for the actual game."

"*I* wouldn't understand. Besides," she enthused, "It's a cool game. I can't wait to play it."

The sparkle that had undone him on Sunday was about to do the same again, if he wasn't careful. "You play video games? Pardon my surprise."

"Video games aren't just for the guys. Don't limit me by your own narrow views."

And for one tantalizing second he could almost see the tomboy who'd traded cheerful insults over cars, could almost see cutoffs and a skinny top instead of the sassy pleated skirt and thoroughly feminine blouse she was wearing today. For a moment he was tempted to clasp her chin, to look for the sprinkling of freckles and the streak of grease.

But she'd already turned away, striding across the grass toward another marker.

Dominic glanced at his watch and cursed silently. He wouldn't be able to check that Ariana was all right if he didn't leave soon.

Lexie had turned his way. "Over here, we'll have—" Her voice broke off when she realized that he hadn't followed her.

Dominic sighed. "I apologize. I will have to get the rest of the tour another time." And he meant it, more than he could say. No matter how often he reminded himself that they had to work together, that he had no time to pursue whatever had happened between them, that this launch was everything to Poseidon, a corner of his heart rebelled at the loss of something he still wasn't sure he hadn't imagined.

But it wasn't his lot in life to pursue his own

pleasures, not when so many others depended upon him to keep his head on straight.

Besides, from what he saw, she couldn't care less. From the moment they'd been introduced in his office, the tomboy he might have only imagined had vanished as if she never existed.

"No problem," she said, her face composed and still. "If I need anything, I can contact Mr. Stafford, I assume."

No, Lexie. Fierce and sudden, the determination arose. *I don't want you to need Bradley. I want you to need me.*

It's my own damnable luck that I cannot afford to need you.

"That's right," he responded, turning away. "Bradley can handle whatever you need."

"I'll stay out of your way as much as possible. Am I permitted to speak to your sister?" Her voice could have cut glass.

He turned back. "My sister is very fragile right now. I won't have you upsetting her."

"Your sister is lonely. Even a perfect stranger can see that." Her chin tilted upward.

Her accusation stung. "I do not need your help, Ms. Grayson. I will thank you to stay out of matters you don't understand." He was doing everything in his power to heal Ariana's wounded heart, and he didn't need a stranger to tell him he was failing.

"If she speaks to me, I'm not ignoring her." Defiant green eyes challenged him. Aroused him. Made him want to tell the world to go to the devil while he covered the distance between them and grabbed her, forced her to admit what they'd shared.

But she looked as likely to spit in his eye as to admit to anything.

And he had a crucial meeting to attend.

"Be careful with my sister, Ms. Grayson. You can be replaced."

Shock flashed across her features, chased by hurt.

Dominic cursed silently at the temper he'd thought long ago mastered. "Lexie—" One hand lifted from his side.

She set her shoulders very straight. It only emphasized her fragility. She was such a contrast, so delicate and so strong.

But there was nothing fragile about her icy voice. "You've made yourself quite clear. If you'll excuse me, I must get back to work." She turned her back and walked away.

He watched her go, frowning. Wondering how his normally sharp instincts had let him down so badly.

She'd seemed so different, that Sunday that had been only three days ago but seemed a part of some other universe now.

She hadn't known who he was then. She knew now, and just as always, it had changed everything.

The Dominic who had perfected the art of putting his responsibilities ahead of his wishes, knew it was right to do that now. A treasure hunt for a mirage was a luxury he didn't have.

No matter how much his heart wished otherwise.

Dominic let out a sigh torn from his depths. Then he shook off foolish wishes and headed for the house.

Chapter Four

"Max?" Lexie called. "You here?" She entered their shared studio in an old warehouse near the railroad tracks overlooking Town Lake, torn between hoping he wasn't...and needing the comfort of her old friend.

No answer. She headed for the coffeepot, seeing it reduced to sludge but still on. He was here, just obsessed. As usual. Lost deep inside that imaginary world of his mind.

She started a fresh pot, then went to his door and there he was, hunched over his computer, playing her like a lover. Max's computer was named Maisie, and woe betide the person who didn't believe she was real. Max certainly did.

For a moment she stood in the doorway, shaking her head. Most people thought of computer dweebs, as Max called himself and his friends, as little nerdy guys with thick glasses and pocket protectors. Max was anything but. A lean six feet tall with a leonine mane of golden hair and crystalline-blue eyes, he was forever making women stop and stare.

She'd asked herself why she didn't fall for him. The answer was simple—she loved Max far too much to make that mistake. He was big brother/father figure/best friend all rolled up in one package. Love could ruin a great friendship.

Max felt the same way, she knew, forever nagging her to date more, fixing her up with all manner of men. He kept thinking he'd change Lexie's mind, but he was wrong. When you invested too much emotion in a man, you were in trouble. That's when you made yourself vulnerable…and when you'd get hurt. Her father had told her he loved her, then one day he'd left and never returned. After her mother's death, a scared, lonely Lexie had finally succumbed to her college boyfriend's declarations of love, given him her virginity, then gotten a call a month later that he was going to marry his high school sweetheart.

Men said they loved you and they left. Lexie liked men, enjoyed their company a great deal, but she wouldn't be a fool again. Friendship was great. Love sucked. The little white house with the picket fence was a lovely dream, but it happened to other people, not to her.

The other night was a perfect example.

When you screw up, Lexie, you do it big.

Resolutely, Lexie turned away and went back to the kitchen area, snagging a cup of coffee for herself and filling Max's Batman mug. She tiptoed toward his desk and slipped it onto the coaster beside him.

Max jerked in surprise, then smiled. "Hey," he greeted her. Then he frowned. "You look different. What happened?"

"Nothing." Nothing she could discuss. She sipped her coffee. "What are you working on?"

Max smirked. "Like you care. Every time I try to explain my software, you start falling asleep."

"I do not—" She grinned. "Actually, I think I used the word *coma.*"

"Maybe this won't put you in a coma. Have I ever shown you my Easter egg?"

Lexie frowned. "Easter egg?"

"Sort of like a watermark on paper. It's an image I bury to mark this program as mine. If you know the right keystrokes to use—" He hit a series of keys, and up popped an image of his old beat-up van. Lexie blinked in surprise.

Max grinned. "See? Magic."

She was still staring at the image. "How did you do that?"

"Here—stay awake and watch this. It's just six keystrokes."

Lexie watched carefully, grateful for the distraction from her misery. She tried it herself, ridiculously pleased when it worked. "Did you put it in the program that you think Poseidon stole?"

His eyes darkened. "Yeah."

"If you haven't seen Poseidon's graphics, why do you suspect them?"

"Some gamers were in a chat room, debating theories on speeding up graphics. One of them was bragging about an amazing algorithm in software they were using on a new game."

"What's an algorithm?"

One brow lifted. "You really want to know?"

She managed a weak smile. "Not really."

Max's brows drew together. "Anyway, he called the algorithm 'Einstein's marble.'"

She frowned. "That's important?"

He nodded. "I created Einstein's marble. It's the basis of my method. So I've been nosing around, asking questions behind the safe anonymity of cyberspace, and when I put the pieces together along with the buzz on Poseidon's new game, I'm almost certain that's what happened."

"How did they steal it?"

"Ever heard the term 'hacker'?"

Even she had heard of that. "How did they know you had it?"

Max's color deepened. "I've wracked my brains to figure that out. Best I can guess is that something I said online piqued someone's interest, and they got past my firewalls. I've taken extra precautions since.''

''So what do you do about Poseidon?''

''Unless I can get some firepower on my side, I wait until the game comes out.''

''What kind of firepower?''

''Preferably a shark lawyer.'' He paused for a beat. ''If I had any money.''

''Why don't you just confront Poseidon?''

''They're too big. They'd just stall me while they buried the evidence.''

''But—'' she protested.

He pinned her with a solemn stare. ''I can't be hasty about this, Lex. If I get impulsive, I'll lose for sure. Every step has to be thought out. Most of all, I need proof, more than just some guys bragging in a chat room.''

It was so unfair that he didn't have the money to take on a giant such as Poseidon. Had she met the man who might have stolen his dreams—and fallen into bed with him that same night? A stubborn part of her still wanted to believe that her Nikos existed. *That* man would never have—

''Hello?'' Max snapped his fingers. ''What's wrong?''

''Nothing.''

''Kid, don't ever play poker. Your face tells everything.'' He was always calling her ''kid.'' He was only thirty-one, two years older than she was.

She'd have to tell him something or he'd never

leave her alone. She shrugged, and forced a casualness to her tone. "Just a hard day."

He studied her too closely but, to her relief, he didn't push for more. "You hungry?"

"Not really."

"Well, I am. Come on—you can keep me company. We'll go to Hut's. I'll even buy." Without waiting for an answer, he headed for the door, assuming she'd follow.

Lexie admitted to herself that the last thing she wanted was to return to the dome, with all its memories, so though she wasn't hungry, she fell in behind Max. Five minutes later, they'd walked the two blocks to their favorite hangout.

Hut's Hamburgers was an institution in Austin dating back to the 1950s, and nothing about it had changed since long before Lexie had first come here ten years ago. Still the same linoleum floor, still the same mementos on the walls…still jammed full every day of the week with patrons from across the spectrum.

"Ah, grease…" Max sighed. "There's something about the smell of a grill and French fries sizzling in artery-clogging glory."

A laugh bubbled up from Lexie's throat, and it felt wonderful. Here was something solid, something familiar.

Max waited until they'd given their drink order, then pounced. "Okay, spill it. Tell me what's wrong."

Lexie tried for casual. "I met someone, that's all. Or thought I did."

"*Someone?*" He leaned closer, staring. "You never meet *someone.* Guys hit on you and you never notice. I try to fix you up with guys who could become *someone*—you run like a rabbit at the first sign of the real thing."

"What would you know about the real thing, Max Lancaster? You never date a woman more than once."

He lifted an eyebrow. "We're not talking about me." He cocked his head, then whistled softly. "Son of a gun. You did it, didn't you? You met a guy who got past the wall."

Lexie wanted so badly to tell him everything. She'd never hidden a thing from Max before—but she didn't know whom she'd met. Just that she'd never felt that way before—ever.

"Lex—" Max's tone was serious now. "Talk to me."

She met his gaze and was shocked to feel tears brimming. "He was incredible, Max," she whispered. "I've never—"

Max clasped her hand across the table. "Oh, hell, kid. I always knew you'd fall like a ton of bricks one day. Who is he?"

"I didn't fall for anyone," she protested. Then she burst into tears. "He was gone when I woke up, Max."

Max's voice turned deadly, like the big brother

she'd always wanted. "That's it. I'll kill him. What's his name?"

She couldn't tell him. She was too ashamed of being a fool. And truthfully, she didn't know whom she'd met that night. Certainly not the cold stranger who owned Poseidon. She would never have given that man a second look.

"I don't know," she whispered.

He shook his head slowly. "Good God." He squeezed her hand tighter, his eyes filled with concern.

After a minute or two Lexie pulled away, sniffing hard. Max pulled a handkerchief from his pocket and offered it. She accepted gratefully.

"So what are you going to do?" he asked.

"What can I do?" She pasted on a smile. "I feel like such a fool." He couldn't know how much.

"Don't beat yourself up, Lex." Max glanced uneasily toward where he'd last seen the waitress.

Lexie stifled an honest laugh. Like most guys, Max would rather take a bullet than deal with tears. "You've done your friend duty. I'm fine now. No more tears, I promise."

She was surprised to find out it was true. She did feel better. Her best friend and comfort food—what more could anyone want? Suddenly she was ravenous. "I want onion rings, a shake—the works, Max. This is gonna cost you."

He grinned and shrugged. "I'm not sure if I ate

today, so I'll just consider that you're saving my life—and that, my friend, is priceless.''

Lexie laughed again, and somehow she felt stronger. More hopeful. She could do this. Max was, indeed, priceless. Their friendship had gotten both of them through many hard times, living off Chinese noodles for weeks on end, scraping every penny to make their dreams happen.

But the thought sobered her. Her dream was happening, but Max's had been stolen.

By Dominic Santorini.

Even as she thought it, she didn't want to believe it. ''Max, would your Easter egg be enough proof of the theft?''

''It would be a start.''

His blue eyes fixed on hers. ''Why are you asking, Lex?'' Then his gaze narrowed. ''No. No way. You're not considering doing something stupid at Poseidon, are you?''

''Well, I—''

''Don't even think about it. This is my problem, and I'll work it out. Don't you dare jeopardize your contract with them, trying to be my champion. You've worked too hard to get this shot.''

''So have you.''

''Stop thinking what you're thinking—right now, you hear me?'' When she didn't answer, he leaned closer. ''Look, you're the best friend I ever had, but I'm a big boy. I'll work this out.''

''But, Max—'' She glanced away, trying to marshal her arguments for why it made sense for her to snoop around.

Her gaze strayed to the hall beside the bar toward the couple just then walking by—

And every thought fled as she met Dominic Santorini's piercing stare.

Oh, my word. Dominic and Ariana. What were they doing here? Slumming?

"Lex, what's wrong?"

She couldn't speak. Just then, Ariana spotted her and waved, then pulled at Dominic's sleeve. Lexie tensed, wishing she could somehow vanish.

But it was too late. Dark eyes fixed on her, he turned to follow his sister.

"You look like you've seen a ghost—" Max craned to see what was spooking her, then whistled. "Well, well, the big boss man himself. I saw Santorini once, speaking at a conference."

"Max, you won't—"

His jaw flexed. "Relax, Lex. I'll play it cool. I'm not about to tip my hand until I'm sure." A dangerous glee danced in his eyes. "But I wouldn't mind an introduction to the babe who's with him. Know her?"

Lexie could barely speak. "She's his sister."

Tawny eyebrows lifted. "How interesting."

"Max, she's—" And then it was too late. Ariana was almost beside her.

The raven hair swung around Ariana's shoulders, and one pair of dark eyes glowed with pleasure.

"Lexie, I am very glad to see you. I don't know anyone in Austin yet, so it is a wonderful surprise to see someone familiar."

Lexie darted a glance at the other set of dark eyes, as stormy as Ariana's were pleased. Heart thumping at the warning there, she rose and hugged the woman. "Hello, Ariana. I'm glad to see you, too."

She turned and gestured toward Max, who had already risen to his feet, his eyes fixed on Ariana. "This is my friend, Max Lancaster. Max, meet Ariana and Dominic Santorini."

Max shook Dominic's hand, and Lexie had to admire his aplomb, knowing that Max probably wanted to rip into Dominic's throat. "Santorini."

Dominic nodded just as curtly, his eyes barely moving from Lexie's face. "My pleasure."

It felt like a spotlight, his gaze. If she'd been a bug on a pin, she couldn't have been more uncomfortable, even avoiding meeting his eyes as she was.

"Ms. Grayson, it is a surprise to see you again so soon."

She dared a glance at him, then wished she hadn't. There was something hot and angry in his gaze.

How dare he? She wasn't the one who'd lied, wasn't the one who'd been so rude this afternoon.

Max broke the moment by reaching for Ariana's hand. "Ms. Santorini, whatever brings you to Austin is welcome indeed." He lifted her hand to his lips with his practiced charm, and Lexie wanted to smack him.

She didn't have to. Ariana withdrew her hand quickly, her cheeks flaring bright red. "I'm visiting my brother."

One look in those anguished eyes and a look of chagrin crossed Max's face. "I only meant to say that you brighten this little backwater." He withdrew carefully, and an awkwardness filled the air.

"Well, I—" Lexie desperately wanted to keep Max from noticing the charge leaping between her and Dominic. She could barely breathe.

"We had better take our seats." Dominic rescued them all. "Lancaster, good to meet you." He nodded and turned toward Lexie. "Ms. Grayson, I'd like to meet with you again and straighten out some details."

He was surely talking about the gala plans, but she couldn't be certain. Those black eyes raked her just short of indecency. And the heat and anger hadn't cooled.

She was all too aware of Max's curious glance and Ariana's perusal. She swallowed hard. "I thought you wanted me to coordinate with Mr. Stafford from now on."

"I changed my mind." The deep voice was as much command as explanation. "Call my secretary tomorrow and let me know when you are available. I will do my best to accommodate your schedule."

She needed this job. Surely at his office he wouldn't—

"Yes, all right," she stammered. "You're the boss." She couldn't meet his gaze again, too afraid Max would put two and two together, too worried about being alone with Dominic.

So she glanced at Ariana instead. "I'm glad to see you again, Ariana. I hope you enjoy the food here."

"Thank you. I hope you'll be at the house again soon, Lexie."

Lexie cut a glance at Dominic's forbidding countenance, very aware of his dictate that she leave his sister alone.

He might be able to order her around when it came to this job, but if Ariana wanted to talk, she'd listen. Lexie knew all about being lonely. "I'll look forward to it."

She smiled brightly, defiantly. Dominic scowled.

Dominic ushered Ariana to a table in the corner, seating her with her back to the room so that he could take the chair with the view of Lexie and the tall, blond man with whom she was so intimate.

His teeth ground together as he heard Lexie's delighted laughter. He fought the urge to walk back over and smash his fist into Max Lancaster's face—

Simply because Lexie laughed with him as she once had so freely shared her laughter with a man named Nikos. Because her hand had been clasped in Max Lancaster's and not his own.

"I'm so happy to see Lexie again. I really like her—" Ariana glanced up from her menu and every bit of pleasure fled from her face. "What's wrong?"

He realized that he was frowning. Hard. Glaring toward Lexie's companion. "Nothing." He straightened, picked up his menu, tried to make sense of the words.

"Nothing? Dominic, we may have spent most of our lives apart, thanks to my mother's deceit, but a perfect stranger could tell you're upset about something." Then she hit too close to home. "You were upset this afternoon at the house. You don't like Lexie?" Her face showed how incomprehensible that was.

And just how much his vaunted self-control slipped every time Lexie was around. No one had ever gotten under his skin the way she did, and the distraction she presented was unsettling. Dangerous.

If only he could find his way back to the tomboy, but that woman had vanished like mist in the noonday sun.

His sister's face bore not the smiles he'd hoped to generate by bringing her here tonight, but confusion and sorrow. "I am sorry. It has nothing to do with her." It was only partly a lie. "There are matters at the company—"

Ariana reached across the table to grasp his hand. "You can talk to me, Dominic. I care about you, and you've been so good to me when I've made such a mess of my life. Let me do something useful. I can listen, and I'll never say a word. I worry about you because you're so alone.''

Dominic recoiled. He'd always been alone. He preferred it. "Do not worry about me, Ariana. Just concentrate on getting well."

"No man is an island, brother. We are not meant to be alone. All of us need someone to trust, someone to love."

Just then, Lexie and Max rose from their table and made their way to the door, Max's arm slung around Lexie's shoulders.

Her best friend, eh? Inside Dominic an ugly barb twisted. "Trust is a dangerous conceit, little one. Love is even worse. I do better alone." Then he smiled and squeezed her fingers to take the sting out of his words. "But I do appreciate that you care. I'm fine. I am simply more accustomed to solitude." He broadened his smile into one he hoped was convincing. "The French fries here are fresh, not frozen. They are an excellent example of the highest form of American decadence—shall we have some?"

Though Ariana's eyes remained troubled, her lips curved into a smile he welcomed. "Let's have a lot."

Chief among his responsibilities was this tender creature. No longing, however fervent, could be allowed to jeopardize those who depended upon him.

"Your wish is my command."

* * *

What a long day it's been, Lexie thought the next day as she drove back toward Poseidon headquarters near dark. The afternoon meeting had been a long but productive one with two new clients who'd sought her out when they'd heard she was doing the Poseidon gala. Dinner was only a dream; she'd throw together an omelet when she got home.

Bradley had okayed this visit to the game's designers, telling her that they worked odd hours, mostly at night. She needed to check her designs against the final game images. Most people wouldn't notice, but to her, details were everything. And if she could find any evidence—

"Evening, miss." The security guard nodded as she signed in.

"Good evening, Mr—" She squinted at his badge. "Mr. Carlyle. You doing okay tonight?"

"Call me Bob. I can't complain." He grinned. "Wouldn't help if I did."

"Is it hard, working nights?"

"Nah. Better than being at home. The nights get long since my wife passed."

"I'm so sorry."

"It's all right. Been a year now. I'm gettin' used to being alone." His eyes darkened. "Still miss her, though."

"I'll bet." Lexie wanted to sit right here and just visit with him, instead of going forward. Maybe that was better. Maybe fate had put him here just to stop her from making a mistake—

"Well, enough about me. You go on with your plans now. Have a good evening, Ms. Grayson."

"Lexie. And thank you." But she wanted to beg to stay. It was only nerves. She wasn't planning to do anything definite, just keep her eyes open to see if she could find out anything that might help Max.

But she couldn't stop scenarios running through her ever-fertile imagination, scenes where the nice man behind her read her intentions and suddenly shock troops surrounded the place, yelling through bullhorns for her to come out with her hands up, just before the glass started exploding out of the windows.

She grinned at her own foolishness, shrugged her shoulders and went in search of the gamesters, using her badge and thumbprint as she had before to gain entrance.

Portfolio under her arm, she knocked. The door opened upon a familiar scene. Though the actual setup differed by an order of magnitude from Max's hangout in their shared workspace, the tone of the place put her immediately at ease.

These people were every bit as crazed as Max and his crowd.

"Hi. I'm Lexie Grayson. I'm the designer for the launch gala for Legend Quest."

She looked closer and realized that this was a boy,

not a man who'd opened the door. If he was fifteen, she'd be surprised.

"Josh Logan."

"Hi, Josh. May I come in?" He was still standing in the doorway.

"Oh—yeah, sure." He blushed. "Sorry." He moved back and gestured her in, his movements the gangly metamorphosis of a boy approaching manhood, one foot in each camp.

"I like your game."

"Yeah?" He blushed again. "Well, it's not mine. I mean, I was part of it and all, but we had a whole team."

"I'd like to go over my drawings with you, to be sure the final product at the gala will be as close as I can make it."

"Me?" His voice broke. "Well, sure, I mean—"

"Do you have your own workspace?"

"Yeah." He remained where he was.

"Perhaps we could go there," she nudged gently.

"Oh—yeah. Right. This way."

She didn't even know the names for much of what she saw. Computer equipment everywhere, with vivid game scenes on the monitors—the place seemed utterly chaotic. Paper airplanes hung from the ceiling, but airplanes more wacky than any she'd ever constructed. The man nearest the door sat at a desk with a huge stuffed purple ape hanging over his partition. Someone had been to Mardi Gras—the poor ape's color could barely be seen for the weight of all the sparkling bead throws draped around his neck.

She wasn't really surprised when no one noticed her entrance. She'd spent years feeding Max and his gang while they puzzled over this problem and that. Periods of frenetic activity would be succeeded by periods in which everyone in the room seemed to enter hibernation and vacant stares became the order of the day.

"Nice place." She turned to Josh, only to find him drifting toward his workspace again. She followed him, and though he blushed furiously every other minute, he was soon absorbed in showing off the wonders of their creation.

Lexie waved goodbye an hour and a half later, but their heads were already turning back toward the problems they'd been contemplating when she arrived. Good thing—it was all she could do to keep quiet.

In some ways, she'd gotten what she came for; she was satisfied that her designs would work beautifully. But she'd also gotten a few moments alone when Josh left his computer to answer a question from one of his cohorts. Heart pounding out of her chest, Lexie had tried out Max's keystrokes, but as she was hitting the last one, she'd glanced up to see Josh returning. She'd panicked and fumbled for the escape key just as what might have been Max's Easter egg blinked on—and as quickly vanished.

She could almost believe she'd imagined it...but she was afraid she had not.

Oh, Nikos—

Heart aching, lost in thought, she was halfway down a darkened hallway when she realized she'd made a wrong turn. She was in the executive wing. Only two lights shone through doorways down the hall; from one of them, she heard a voice. Eager to find her way out of this creepy hallway quickly, she headed toward it, hoping to get assistance.

As she approached, she realized it was Bradley Stafford's voice she heard, and her feet slowed. She wasn't altogether comfortable being in a deserted hallway with him. He was always polite but she sensed an undercurrent of dislike, though she didn't know why. As she stood there, debating, he slammed down the phone, and she heard him sigh loudly. His footsteps sounded, heading in her direction.

She jumped into action, moving down the hallway. She couldn't deal with him now, not after finding out that Dominic—

"Ms. Grayson? What are you doing here?"

Too late. She turned as if toward a firing squad. *Steady, Lexie. You're just lost. Remember that.*

Resolutely, she widened her eyes. "Oh, Mr. Stafford—thank heavens. I went to see the game gurus and took a wrong turn somewhere. I'm so lost I can barely keep track of myself," she chattered.

He frowned at her. "How did you get over here in this wing?"

"I wish I knew. I have the worst habit of day-dreaming and before I knew it, I looked up and had no idea where I was. This is a confusing layout."

He looked skeptical, so she continued brightly. "I wish I'd known this was where your office was. I'd have come straight to you to help me." *Stop chattering, Lexie.* Max had always told her she'd be hopeless at poker.

He looked at her, long and hard, then rubbed his face with one hand, his fatigue showing. He wasn't so dapper-looking now.

"You look tired. Why don't you go home?" she asked.

"I plan to do that as soon as I help you find your way back to the entrance."

"Oh, I'm fine. Just point me in the right direction."

His eyes narrowed, his usual aplomb missing. "As you might imagine, we are not fond of outsiders wandering the facilities." He took her arm, and Lexie wanted to shake him off. His grip held firm.

He gestured for her to precede him down the hallway. "Please, Ms. Grayson. I insist."

Like a doomed prisoner or a chastened child, Lexie went quietly, hoping he couldn't hear the pounding of her heart.

Or the breaking.

* * *

He should apologize. He would do that as soon as she called about her schedule.

Why hadn't she called, damn it?

Dominic spun his chair around, away from the work he couldn't seem to concentrate on, and stared out across the hills, seeing nothing but a sky-blue dome dotted with clouds, hearing the creak of chains holding a swinging bed.

Why, out of all the women he'd known, could he not forget this one? She wasn't who she'd seemed that first day. That night that was seared into his brain.

Do you believe in magic, Nikos?

For one unforgettable night, he had.

He should have it out with her. Now. Ask her, straight-out, why finding out who he was had changed everything.

But he couldn't. Didn't want to. He didn't want those memories to die completely. Didn't want to face that the magical sprite had vanished forever in the clear light of day. He couldn't pursue anything between them right now, even if he could bridge the crevasse that widened between them with every passing hour.

Dominic had never been a coward, never been afraid to face harsh, naked truths. His life had been filled with a lot of them, but the truth he would find if he forced Lexie to talk about that night...he wasn't ready to face. She might be an apparition, that luscious tomboy who'd set his blood on fire, who'd made him laugh, who'd made him feel years younger and carefree.

But right now, while he was fighting for the life of the company that was his only child...while he fought for the soul of his sister...

He needed that apparition, that hope. Losing it would rob him of something essential, something he'd thought impossible to find amid all the people who wanted him for what he had, not who he was.

So he would make amends with Lexie, but he wouldn't ask. Wouldn't talk about that night he'd tucked away for safekeeping.

But one day, when this was all over, when Poseidon was safe, when Ariana was stronger—

He would drive back to that dome to see if he could find the tomboy.

Dominic heaved a deep sigh and was turning back to his work when the knock came. "It's open."

Bradley opened the door.

"Good morning—" Dominic looked harder. "What's wrong?"

Bradley stared at him for a moment. "Maybe nothing."

"What does that mean?"

Bradley shook his head. Still he paused. "What's up between you and Ms. Grayson?"

Dominic didn't answer immediately. Bradley was his best friend, but there were some things he wasn't prepared to discuss with anyone. "Why do you ask?"

Bradley shut the door and crossed toward him. "You've acted strangely both times you've been around her. That's not like you."

"There is much going on. We are both tired, Bradley. Perhaps you read too much into my actions. Ms. Grayson has a contract with us, and her work is crucial to a success we need very much." He shrugged as if that were all there was to it. "I am very concerned. Perhaps I have not been as diplomatic as I could."

"We could move the launch date. Hire someone else."

"Why would you say that? What has happened?"

Bradley glanced away. "Maybe nothing."

He rounded his desk. "Don't do that. Talk to me."

His friend eyed him carefully. "I'm not sure. There may be something funny going on. I'm just not certain she should be working on the gala."

"What?" Dominic stared, jamming his fists into his pockets, clenching and unclenching them. "Why?"

"There has to be an inside connection to our troubles, don't you agree?"

Dominic nodded.

Bradley shook his head. "She was up at the office late last night, visiting with the design crew. I found her in our hallway. I had a sense she might be eavesdropping outside my door."

Dominic's stomach churned. No. He didn't want

to hear the rest, but he had to. "You're sure she was eavesdropping?"

"Oh, hell, I'm not sure. I was so damn tired. She said she got lost, but—" Bradley frowned.

"Lexie doesn't know anything about our business."

"Lexie, is it?" Bradley's eyes narrowed. "She knows more about Legend Quest than anyone outside this organization."

"No. She would never—" Dominic stopped, aware that Bradley was studying him curiously. He backtracked. "I do not see how she would have the knowledge to do anything harmful."

"Suit yourself." Bradley shrugged. "I just don't like it. There was something about her last night, something frenetic, almost guilty." Then he shook his head. "Perhaps it was just as she said, she merely got lost."

But he didn't think so, that much was clear.

Who was Lexie, really? Either she was for real, or she was the best liar Dominic had ever met. He shook his head in anguished confusion. If she was for real, then why had she done such an about-face? If she was a liar, how could he have mistaken her sweetness in the act of love?

As he fought to retain a sense of Lexie, his doubts swamped in to overload it. He wanted to rush to her right now and demand an explanation. He'd force it out of her if he had to—

He felt sick. He closed his eyes. He couldn't care

so much about a liar. He couldn't fall for a woman who'd deceive and betray him.

But he knew he could. He'd done it before.

Celia. The name still made his gut twist. She'd said she loved him...said he was her world...said they'd build a life together.

Then she'd stolen information from his fledgling company and run to a competitor with it. He had sworn he would never trust his heart again. And look what he had almost done.

"No," he growled. "We won't fire her. We will keep her close where we can watch her every move."

Chapter Five

Lexie was hard at work sketching a sudden inspiration as the crew staked out the final location of the set. She didn't have a lot of time today. Tonight was the Starlight Ball and she'd been juggling the two jobs for days. She'd decided that her meeting with Dominic later would go better outside with others around where she wouldn't feel so overwhelmed by him. Meeting him alone in his office after what she'd glimpsed on Josh's computer called for a far better poker face than she possessed.

Part of her wanted to just come out and ask Dominic, but part of her wasn't sure she could bear to know. She didn't want to lose the dream of Nikos, and she'd never believe that man could be a thief.

But Dominic Santorini, so powerful, so remote? He was not a man she knew or one she could predict.

It wasn't her place to decide, anyway. It was Max's, and he'd been very clear. *I can't be hasty about this, Lex. If I get impulsive, I'll lose for sure.*

If only he weren't gone on a much needed few days away. He deserved a break, and she couldn't disturb that, not when she wasn't positive. She would keep her eyes and ears open and maybe, just maybe, she'd turn out to be wrong.

She glanced up and saw Ariana standing on the terrace, watching.

"Hi," she called, smiling.

Ariana waved but didn't come closer, her posture uncertain.

Sketch pad still in hand, Lexie walked over to her. "How are you?"

The younger woman's lips curved, though her eyes held shadows. "I'm happy to see you. You're working hard on this hot day." She pointed toward the sketch pad. "What is that?"

"Just a sketch of an idea for a modification that just occurred to me."

Ariana pointed one long, slender finger at a caricature Lexie had sketched in the corner. "That's the blond man over there," she exclaimed, her eyes lighting. "How long did that take you?"

Lexie hadn't even been conscious of drawing the

workman. "A couple of minutes, probably." She grinned. "I doodle while I'm thinking."

"That's unbelievable. Show me." She paused. "I'm sorry. You probably don't have time."

She didn't, but the eagerness that had skipped over Ariana's face was irresistible. "Sure I do. Just keep talking." She began to sketch Ariana in quick, sure strokes.

"What shall I say?" The other woman's gaze drifted downward. "Oh, my goodness—look at that! So quickly—oh, please, can you spare a moment to show Mrs. Garcia?"

"Who's Mrs. Garcia?"

"She's Dominic's housekeeper, but she mothers us both." Her lovely face clouded, but she shook her raven hair and grasped Lexie's hand. "I'll fix you something cool to drink. Oh, this is remarkable—how do you do it?"

Lexie barely had time to answer as she was swept inside.

Dominic arrived home early for the meeting, though he was hardly eager to see Lexie, given Bradley's news. He glanced over at the work crew but didn't see her. He headed inside to get something cool to drink while he tried to assemble the composure that normally came so easily to him.

He didn't want to believe Bradley was right, but there was no question that Lexie had changed toward him once she knew his identity. And it was also true that their troubles had begun around the time Lexie got her contract at Poseidon.

Never in a million years would he believe it of the tomboy—but of the woman who'd taken her place?

He entered through the garage and heard the giggling.

Giggling? He recognized Lexie's laughter immediately, and Mrs. Garcia's, but the other voice? He hadn't heard Ariana laugh like that even once.

As he rounded the corner to the kitchen, he took in several sights at once: Lexie's slender back as she bent over a sketch pad, Ariana craning to watch, Mrs. Garcia's face flushed as she stood still as though modeling.

Facing his direction, Mrs. Garcia spotted him first and all but jumped out of her skin. "Señor Dominic, I didn't hear you. Come, you must see what the *señorita* can do."

Ariana whirled, her eyes shining with a joy he'd thought never to see. "Oh, Nikos, look what Lexie can do!" She pulled at his arm to bring him closer.

Lexie stepped away and faced him, guilt and distress chasing across her face, the sketch pad held tightly against her breasts. "I'm sorry. I lost track of the time," she stammered.

"Do Nikos, Lexie. Look, Nikos—" Ariana pointed at the surface of the sketch pad, which Lexie was still holding in a death grip.

"May I?" he asked, curiosity overcoming discomfort at having walked into a cozy scene where he felt like the outsider.

"I—I guess." With obvious reluctance, she surrendered the pad.

On it was a quick sketch of Mrs. Garcia that caught her perfectly, that somehow captured her motherly nature as well as her innate pride and strength.

He glanced at Lexie. "This is very good."

"Look at the one before it—I can't believe what she can do in only a few minutes." Ariana's shiny dark hair swung as she reached forward to flip the page.

Beside him, Dominic could feel Lexie's presence as though he stood next to a fire. With only half his attention, he tried to focus on the page flipping forward.

He frowned. "Astonishing." Ariana was there on the sheet, in two poses. One revealed the wounded creature he'd been trying to protect—

The other was the Ariana who was with them now, nothing short of a miracle. Laughter sparked in her eyes, her face relaxed in pleasure. Lexie had captured the young woman he'd lost hope of retrieving.

He turned to glance at Lexie, only to find her green eyes fixed on him, a blush staining her cheeks, hiding the freckles he'd kissed, one by one, on that star-filled night.

For a moment it was as though time stopped, as

did his breath. Longing flooded him—and white-hot
desire. He gripped the sketch pad so tightly he heard
the paper crinkle.

"Draw Nikos, Lexie," Ariana begged. "Please,
Nikos, it will only take a minute."

Dominic ripped his gaze away from Lexie, tearing
away the tender skin of memories that haunted him
still. "Ariana—" But then he looked at his sister,
at the glow on her face, and knew that he'd do anything to keep it there.

He turned back to Lexie, carefully closing a mask
over his feelings. "Perhaps you do not have time,
but if you can spare it, I would like to do this for
Ariana."

Surprise flickered in those green eyes that dogged
his nights. "I—I suppose, if you have the time…"

"What must I do?"

She shook her head as if waking up. "Nothing.
Just…stand there."

"I do not know how to be a model."

Lexie chewed on her lip as she thought about having him model. Remembered what she'd tried so
hard to forget: the hard angles and planes of his
muscular body. The image of her pirate. More than
once, she'd picked up the sketch pad to record that
very image, hoping to exorcise it from her brain.

She didn't answer him. Instead, she concentrated
on her pencil and simply drew.

"May I?" Ariana moved to her shoulder and

gasped. Mrs. Garcia moved to Lexie's other side. *"¡Madre de Dios!"* she said.

Lexie glanced up at Dominic again, only to be caught in his gaze, a stare so hot and hungry, she felt faint.

The pencil point broke beneath the pressure of her clenched fingers. She jerked her gaze from his and all but threw the sketch pad down. "Excuse me, please. I'll be outside when you're ready."

And she fled.

Dominic itched to go after her, but the two women were staring at him as though he were a monster.

"What's wrong?" Ariana asked. "Nikos, why is it you frighten Lexie so?"

He had no answers, not for Ariana, not for himself. "I will be outside."

"Wait—" Ariana grabbed the sketch pad and turned it in his direction.

A pirate rose from the page, bold and powerful and deadly dangerous. It was him, all right, the features correct to an astonishing degree—

But it was not a Dominic Santorini anyone had ever seen.

Correction. Anyone but one luscious tomboy.

"Is that how she sees you, Nikos?" Ariana smiled. "A pirate." She turned to Mrs. Garcia, her grin widening. "A swashbuckler, our Dominic. I like it."

Unaccustomed heat flared in his cheeks. "She is

a designer. She makes a living from her imagination.''

The two women traded looks of disbelief.

He exhaled in disgust. ''Think what you wish. I have business to conduct.'' Then he fled outside in search of Lexie, though for one of the few times in his life, he had no idea what to say.

He found her in earnest discussion with a workman. She appeared prepared to stay glued to the man's side for the duration.

''Excuse me,'' he addressed the man. ''I am Dominic Santorini.'' He held out a hand.

''Tom Dorman. Pleased to meet you, Mr. Santorini. Amazing place you got here.''

''I like it.'' But he stared at Lexie as he said it, and knew he lied. He'd trade it all for a dome, a valley, and no responsibilities. ''Please excuse us, Tom. Ms. Grayson and I were scheduled to meet and I'm afraid my time is short.''

''No problem. Got plenty of work to do.'' The man moved away.

Lexie stood perfectly still, quivering like a doe in the sights of a rifle.

She was so small, so delicate. He forgot that because her personality was so big, so expansive.

Around everyone else, at least. And for one special day, she'd been that way around him.

Damn, how he wanted to forget everything else in his life—but that wasn't remotely possible. But he wanted to remind her that they hadn't always had all of this separating them.

"How is Rosebud?"

She startled as if she didn't recognize the name. "Rosebud?"

"Your cat. Small, gray, noisy?" he reminded her.

She looked at him for a moment, and he would have sold his soul to read her mind, to separate the mélange of emotions chasing over her expressive face.

Then as suddenly as they'd come, she locked them away, became Ms. Grayson.

"I'm sorry. I'm juggling two jobs today. If you don't mind—" She turned away and gestured. "The Chamber of Doom will begin over here." With quick steps, she put distance between them.

He didn't want to talk about the damned gala. He wanted to grab her, to shake Ms. Grayson loose. To kiss Lexie.

"Did Bradley give you the set of plans I left yesterday?" she asked.

Bradley. His friend's face rose before him, filled with concern. *She knows more about Legend Quest than anyone outside this organization.* Nonsense. Lexie couldn't be the inside source.

But Bradley had warned him once before, with Celia. Dominic had ignored him, had let the matter drift too long, not wanting to believe his lover could be his betrayer.

And then it had been too late. Poseidon had been

damaged, and Dominic had had to fight his way back to save the people who trusted him from losing their jobs.

He thought about Bob Carlyle the security guard, about Mrs. Murray, about Wally the janitor.

He thought about how he'd never suspected Ariana's mother until she and her lawyer boyfriend had swindled him out of his inheritance. For the sake of the father he had loved, he'd trusted a woman he should have watched.

No matter how sound his judgment was in business, how skilled his instincts, his track record with matters of the heart was deeply flawed. He couldn't afford to be wrong again.

So he simply followed Lexie and resigned himself. "Yes, I read the plans. Show me where the chamber will be."

Dominic walked up the auditorium steps, wishing he were anywhere but at the Starlight Ball tonight, no matter how important the charity. He'd already paid his money and agreed to escort a date who was only a business contact. He felt anything but sociable.

But even so, the surroundings made him take notice. The entrance fed into a tunnel of sorts, a glistening blue-black swirl with enough lighting at floor level to see one's steps, but otherwise giving the sense that one had entered some sort of almost-liquid night. Soft, ethereal music cast an other-worldly spell on the journey. The tunnel curved, and at the end, the faint glow of light beckoned.

"Who did this?" his date murmured. "This benefit has never been done with such imagination."

Dominic remembered Lexie's eagerness to leave to finish another job. He remembered a dome ceiling filled with clouds and tiny stars.

Then they reached the end, where darkness led them into an explosion of starlight.

And he smiled. He'd bet money this was Lexie's work.

The woman beside him gasped. "This is stunning."

It was. The design work was fantastic. Looking at preliminary drawings or pictures of her finished work hadn't done any of it justice.

The Starlight Ball was being held in a star field. Except for the earth beneath their feet, they could have been floating in space, surrounded by a silken net of deepest ink-blue, punctuated by the icy white of millions of stars.

"Incredible." His date shook her head. "Whoever designed this is a genius." She looked up at Dominic. "He should be doing your gala."

She is, Dominic wanted to say. And she is incredible. He glanced around, wondering if she were still here.

"Dominic, I'll be right back. I need to speak to that man over there about a deal we're doing."

He was only too happy to oblige. "You go ahead. I will get us drinks."

He headed for one of the bars dotting the room and smiled as he neared. Each bar was an asteroid, seeming to float above the floor.

Lexie was amazing. She had a gift for whimsy, for seeing things others missed. He'd been wondering again if he'd made a mistake, insisting on keeping her on the Poseidon gala, but tonight answered that question for once and for all. His desire to keep her near, given Bradley's suspicions, might be less than logical, but there was no question that she could do the work they needed. Legend Quest needed her, even if Dominic Santorini couldn't afford to.

He turned, drinks in hand, and headed back, stopping several times to greet fellow executives, trying to not obviously scan the room, but wondering if Lexie was here. Trying to not wish she were.

And then he saw her.

Lexie was still out of breath after a near fall from a ladder while rescuing a cluster of stars that had come unhinged. Climbing a ladder in heels wasn't the smartest move she'd ever made, but it was her design, after all. She didn't want to be out front, anyway. Behind the scenes was fine with her, but as the charity's executive director had pointed out, she could make valuable contacts here by mingling.

She hated mingling. Not with ordinary people, of course. She loved that. But these weren't ordinary

people, these were fat cats who could afford ten-
thousand-dollar-a-person tickets. None of these people drove old pickups or lived in geodesic domes.
Little old Lexie Grayson, who'd never had two pen-
nies to rub together much less two nickels, was out
of her league.

She squeezed her hands into quick fists, then
forced herself to shake off the nerves and suck in a
deep breath. Then she slipped between the panels of
the draping and entered a world where she didn't
belong.

And she couldn't help smiling.

It really did look pretty terrific, if she said so herself.

"You did a stunning job." The deep voice of her
dreams spoke.

Lexie whirled and brushed one of the glasses
Dominic held in his hand.

"I am sorry. I frightened you." He held out one
glass. "You look out of breath."

She ran one hand through her short hair, the
nerves she'd battled off returning and bringing re-
inforcements. "I—I just got off a ladder," she bab-
bled. "A cluster of stars was in the wrong place."

One dark eyebrow rose. He glanced upward.
"One cluster? You could tell that?"

"The creator of any heaven should know where
all her stars are at any given time."

That slashing pirate's grin sent her pulse skipping.
"A good caretaker as well as a gifted creator, I

see.'' He lifted his glass and gently clinked it to hers. ''If I had doubts about the fate of Legend Quest in your hands, tonight would dispense with them. To A. Grayson, designer extraordinaire.''

He took a sip, but she didn't. ''Have you had doubts?''

Shadows returned to his midnight eyes, and she was sorry she'd asked. ''Never mind.'' She glanced around them, desperate for a distraction. ''Where is your date?''

The eyebrow rose again. ''You are so certain I have one?''

''I might not have known you at first, but I've done some reading since then. There are pictures of you everywhere, if only I'd ever taken the time to read the papers or magazines. And you're usually accompanied by some gorgeous, sophisticated woman.''

''If you had known who I was, would you have stopped to help, Lexie?''

She didn't want to have this discussion. Remembering that night edged too closely to things she couldn't bear to consider, questions she didn't dare ask. Her dearest friend was now faced with the impossible task of tackling Goliath, when he didn't even have David's slingshot. The man who stood in front of her was Goliath, not Nikos. She had to keep that in mind.

Dominic studied her. Clad in a slender drape of deep purple from neck to toes, a dainty gold chain circling her hips, she was a knockout. Too easily, he could remember the skin beneath that gown, feel her breasts in his hands, feel the heat of her around him. She was a breathtaking mystery, a woman of many faces.

He pushed at her silence. He had to know. "Will we ever discuss that night?"

Haunted green eyes looked up at him, terror and guilt mingling, and he realized he would never be ready to know that it had all been a ruse, that she had felt nothing of what he had.

"It was a mistake," she whispered. "I can't—I don't want to talk about it." Her gaze pleaded with him. "Let's just forget it, Nikos—Mr. Santorini. I'm your employee, and I have a very big job to complete in a very short time. I need to focus my full attention to do justice to your gala, to give Legend Quest the launch you want."

"Lexie—" He moved a step closer, needing to pull her close, to taste her again, to remind her of magic so explosive that she couldn't possibly believe he'd ever forget it.

Then tears spilled over her lashes, stopping him in his tracks. "Lexie, I—"

"Please," she whispered. "Please—I have to go." She thrust her wineglass in his hand and escaped, quickly lost in the crowd.

Dominic shoved the glasses at a passing waiter and prepared to charge into the crowd after her, ready to throw bodies aside to get to her, to make her listen, to make her see—

What? the voice inside him queried. *What is it that she needs to see? That you have a company in trouble, a sister in need, an old enemy who's jeopardizing them both?*

She'd said, *I need to focus.* On more than the gala? On her efforts to dig out information? To help his enemy hurt him?

No. The man who'd been in her magic kingdom cried out that the Lexie he'd made love to could do no such thing.

But the man who had a company to save shook his head, cleared his eyes of the fog of desire, of longing too strong to trust. He'd seen the nerves, felt her unease. He couldn't dispel the sense that there was something going on with her, something more than this job, more than that night.

It would be irresponsible to ignore that simply because every cell in his body ached for a woman who might not exist.

He needed to focus, too. Every moment around her, his concentration suffered, yet she drew him like a moth to flame.

Somehow he had to resolve this without taking a foolish risk. He had to be sure that his desire to believe her to be the tomboy he wanted back so desperately wasn't overruling his instincts, his vaunted logic.

Dominic Santorini had taken a lot of risks in his

life, but never had he wanted to take one more than now. This was not his risk alone, however, so he would have to approach it with caution. He needed to get to know Lexie better, needed to peer inside her many faces.

He would invite her to the company picnic day after tomorrow. He would watch her closely, observe her interactions with his staff, see if there was a single slip, a sign that she knew anyone too well.

And if inviting her meant that he might also spend more time with her himself, give them a chance to become more at ease around one another—

He would not complain.

Chapter Six

Lexie glanced again at the map Mrs. Murray had given her when she'd conveyed Dominic's invitation to the company picnic. Mrs. Murray had made it clear that attendance was not considered optional, however.

Command performance was more like it.

She didn't want to go. Didn't want to see him again—no, correction. She wanted to see Nikos, wanted to find her way back to that night. It was Dominic Santorini she didn't want to see. He was too big, too powerful, too rich, too...*there*. So strong a presence that all the air in the room vanished when he was near.

And he confused her. She shouldn't have felt the shivers from the mere brush of fingers when he'd handed her the wineglass. She should be able to keep it straight in her head that he'd stolen Max's work. All right, maybe he hadn't stolen it himself, but if she'd learned one thing from spending time at Poseidon, it was that there was nothing too small to escape Dominic's attention. Everyone from the janitor up could detail personal encounters they'd had with the man at the top—and not just him giving orders.

The sense of teamwork at Poseidon was remarkable—everyone at whatever level had a sense of shared mission, had a stake in the company's success. He'd set up a child-care center that was both warm and stimulating, had even created an adult day care for those with aging parents. Both were right on the premises, along with a state-of-the-art fitness center and a cafeteria with food as good as anything she'd ever had.

So somehow he knew—had to know—about Max's software. Yet his manner with her did not smack of guilt.

And now he wanted to discuss that night?

Lexie shook her head violently. She would never be ready to have that discussion. She'd lived down to her mother's worst expectations, thrown caution to the winds—and she'd paid.

Now all that could be done was to pick up the pieces and learn from her mistakes, to go on with as much grace as possible given that Dominic Santorini had seen her lose her mind in his arms.

Lexie looked up too late to catch her turn. Shaking her head, she glanced around for a place to turn.

Please...let there be about a million people here so I can hide and not see him.

Where was she?

"You okay?" Bradley asked.

"Why do you ask?" Dominic continued to scan the resort he'd leased for the day. Sand for beach volleyball, tennis and basketball courts, a small carnival for the children. Horseback riding, croquet, big clumps of shade trees to escape the heat. A dance floor for later.

"You seem preoccupied."

"We do not have ample reason for concern?"

Bradley's jaw hardened. "Of course we do. But you're prowling like a caged beast. Is it Ariana?"

"I wish I could have convinced her to come. She needs to get out more." Dominic turned to his friend. "How was your dinner?"

A muscle in Bradley's cheek ticked. "It was fine."

Dominic remembered that she'd come home early. "Give her time." His own jaw tightened. "That bastard. I will pay him back for what he did. She is a shadow of who she was." His gaze narrowed. "But she will come back, if it is the last thing I accomplish. Lexie made her laugh. It was so good to hear.''

"She's very fond of Lexie. Perhaps too fond." The edge in Bradley's voice sliced into Dominic's conscience.

"We do not know that Lexie is involved with Kassaros. The people I have searching for him have found no trace of a connection." Dominic felt Bradley's gaze on him.

"Do I detect a softening? Have Ms. Grayson's very fine legs obscured your instincts?"

"Do not speak of her like that," Dominic snapped. He met his friend's blue eyes, then glanced away, frowning.

"Dominic…" A note of warning.

He closed his eyes for a second, wondering himself why he couldn't see her clearly. Why his vaunted instincts had gone on holiday. He settled for the easier explanation. "I want my sister to live again, to be free. Lexie is the first person to break through to her." He turned toward Bradley. "So it's complicated."

"No, Dominic. It's very simple. The company is in trouble. Lexie Grayson is the wild card, the woman whose involvement with the company neatly coincided with the first stirrings of trouble. The woman who's made a big fan of young Josh, our genius designer, in case you'd forgotten."

"Enough, Bradley. It is my company, in case you'd forgotten. Poseidon is my blood and bone. I will not risk it or the welfare of its people. I will checkmate Kassaros, but to do that, the launch is critical. The gala is critical. Lexie is crucial to all of that. I am balancing all of it to the best of my ability.'' He glared, knowing as he did it that Bradley's arrows had hit their mark. ''I will manage it. I always have.''

His friend's blue eyes turned cool. He nodded. ''And so you have. Just don't let that woman take up too much of your attention.'' He nodded across the way.

Dominic's head swiveled and he followed Bradley's nod.

There. At last. She'd come, after all.

Mrs. Murray walked over to greet her and the two began to chat as if they were old friends. Bob the security guard walked up to say hello, hand outstretched. Instead, she gave him a quick hug, and Bob beamed with pleasure.

It was the Lexie who would stop to help a stranger. Despite every assurance Dominic had just given his friend, something inside him shifted, opened. Leaned toward the beacon of her presence.

He gave a shrug he didn't feel, for Bradley's sake. Maybe for his own. ''Keep an eye on her. I will do the same.''

''Hey, B.D.,'' Bob said past her shoulder.

Lexie stiffened and tried not to turn to look. She

knew that Dominic's employees teasingly called him "The Big Dog" or "B.D." for short.

"Hello, Bob. Having fun?" the deep voice answered, sending shivers down her spine.

"Oh, yeah. You sure know how to throw a party. I was just trying to convince Lexie here to try a game of horseshoes with me."

Lexie seized on the excuse. "That's great—let's go." She grabbed Bob's arm, ready to race away.

"Want to come along?" Bob asked him.

Say no. Please say no.

"Perhaps I will. I would like to see how Ms. Grayson handles herself." Amusement threaded through that usually very serious voice. "Do you mind?"

She knew it was addressed to her and looked up at him for the first time.

There ought to be a law against the way Dominic Santorini looked in a pair of shorts. Long, tanned, muscular legs. Trim waist, broad shoulders filling a white polo shirt that emphasized his olive skin, his dark, magnetic good looks.

A little short of breath, she summoned up every ounce of grit she possessed. "I've never played before. You might get bored."

Dark eyes held hers in thrall. "I can't imagine anything about you ever being boring, Ms. Grayson."

She hated that *Ms. Grayson* spoken in the slightly accented, deep voice that had the power to make her tremble as memory swept over her. That voice. Those lips…and the things they could do to her…

"Lexie?" Bob spoke up.

She started, having utterly forgotten Bob. Forcing herself back to the moment, she summoned a bright smile, tucking her hand in his elbow. "Right here—and ready if you are."

The older man brightened, the lines of loneliness in his face vanishing. He patted her hand on his arm. "I'll go easy on you." He looked back at Dominic and winked.

"Not on your life, my friend. If I can't win honestly, I'd rather go down in flames."

"A commendable attitude," Dominic said, but there was something odd in his voice.

Lexie glanced over at him as he walked beside her, so tall and proud and commanding. "Honesty is very important to me." *I wish it were to you.*

He held her gaze. "Is it now?"

Lexie frowned at his tone, but just then Bob came to a halt at the horseshoe pit. One of the employees looked up and grinned. "Hey, Bob—just the man I've been waiting for. Come on, let's play."

Bob looked over at Lexie, his gaze uncertain.

Dominic spoke up from beside her. "Why don't you go ahead? I will be happy to answer any questions Ms. Grayson might have."

She wanted to be anywhere but here, but the older man obviously wanted to answer the challenge. "Go ahead," she urged. "I'll watch this round."

"If you're sure…" Bob grinned and headed for the pit, rubbing his hands together.

Lexie stood beside Dominic, feeling the heat from his body even through the heat of the day. He was like a pole to her magnet—a lodestar calling her to him, despite what she knew was wise. She risked a glance upward, only to meet his dark, compelling gaze.

Quickly, she glanced away, but not before she saw amusement light his eyes. She tensed, waiting for him to bring up the subject she'd run away from at the Starlight Ball: their night together. The night of magic that had turned out to be strictly illusion. No substance at all.

Lexie readied herself to make an excuse for why she needed to be elsewhere at this moment. Seek out Mrs. Murray. Powder her nose. Anything, anything at all but having that discussion—or having to lie to this man again.

She hadn't lied when she'd said that honesty was important to her. She'd never been tangled up in anything such as this, and even her intense loyalty to Max lay heavy on her heart. She didn't want to lie to Dominic Santorini; she wanted to come clean, wanted him to come clean. Wanted to spill it all out and devil take the hindmost—

But it was not her dream on the line.

And, truth be told, she wasn't sure she was ready to know if Dominic had played a part. Lexie glanced around for an excuse to get away.

But he surprised her. "Do you see how he holds his horseshoe? His grip is light and easy. The horseshoe will go farther that way." He leaned closer to her and pointed toward Bob with one long finger.

A finger that had trailed over her skin to such devastating effect.

Light-headed, Lexie struggled to answer. "Yes, I—" She cleared her throat of the tightness. "I think I see."

Dominic went on to explain the finer points of the game to her, but all the while, she could smell his scent, that spicy, mysterious scent that was so male, so...Nikos. So entwined with the night of her dreams.

Lexie blinked, trying to follow what he said, but when he placed his hand on the small of her back and bent at the knees to point out something to her, it was all she could do to not press her lips to that strong, tanned throat so tantalizingly close.

Bob threw his arms up in triumph and turned her way, beaming. "Ready, Lexie?"

"Uh, I—" she stammered.

"Come, I will help you." With a small nudge to her back, Dominic urged her forward, the heat of his palm searing through her shirt.

Panic skittered through her. Surely everyone could see how he affected her, could sense how easily he got under her skin, so magnetic, so very unforgettable.

Lexie forced herself to smile at Bob and picked

up her pace, moving away from Dominic's hand. She reached her position past the other pole several steps ahead of him, but just as she bent to grasp her horseshoes, his longer reach seized them, too.

Their hands clasped on the same iron curve, and the feel of him jolted her. She glanced up at him, wondering if he felt it, too. He must be used to bowling women over. She expected to see triumph.

But his eyes were almost sad. A little haunted.

Quickly she glanced away, confused. Uneasy. Wanting too much to reach out to him to soothe the distress she saw there.

"Allow me to show you what I meant." His voice was strictly neutral.

When she glanced at him again, his face was the mask she'd come to expect. Lexie stepped back and yielded the pit to him.

With strong, easy grace, he threw the first shoe and sent it ringing around the pole at the opposite end. The crowd that had gathered cheered, and even Bob was grinning at him. On their faces, she could see the respect, the admiration. He was a winner, and he'd made winners of all of them.

But instead of accepting the cheers as his due, he gestured toward Bob to take his turn, shrugging. "I have heard much of Bob's skill. I can only claim the old saying, 'Better to be lucky than good.'" With his easy manner, he gave Bob the stage instead of accepting it himself.

It was hard to not like a man so confident that he

didn't need to prove himself at anyone else's expense. No wonder his employees were so devoted.

"Now—" He gestured. "Ms. Grayson?"

Good thing she wasn't shy. Instead she grinned at the people gathered around. "Everyone might want to move back. I'm afraid I was the kind of softball pitcher who beaned the batters."

Laughter rippled around the circle, and even Dominic chuckled. Lexie glanced over, struck by the beauty of his smile.

This smile reached all the way to his eyes, and she had seen it only once before. She would never forget it, yet she feared it would never again be directed at her.

He stepped behind her, clasping her waist lightly with one hand and grasping her wrist with the other. "Here, perhaps I can assist in protecting some of my very valuable staff." The smile in his voice rendered an already attractive man too devastating by half.

"Grip it loosely," he murmured next to her ear.

Lexie tried to loosen her death grip, but any sort of relaxation with him this close was asking the impossible. Yet she didn't really want to ask him to move away. She should, but she didn't want to.

Maybe, just for this day, we don't have to be at odds.

So Lexie took a deep breath, trying to focus— until she felt his hand tighten on her waist and heard his own indrawn breath.

How was a girl supposed to concentrate on a game when a man the likes of Dominic Santorini had his hands on her?

"Would you please step back?" she murmured under her breath.

"Why?" he murmured back, and there was mischief in his voice.

Mischief? Dominic?

She whipped her head around, meeting his grin. "Dirty pool, Mr. Santorini. Whose side are you on?"

"Bothering you, Ms. Grayson?" His face was all innocence.

"Not a bit." Lexie smiled, baring her teeth and leaning closer. "Now step back, if you value your life."

He chuckled, but he stepped away, lifting his hands at his sides.

Lexie tried to block out everyone around her, tried to focus on the pole. She closed her eyes, took a deep breath, then opened them and sent the horseshoe flying.

Bob leaped away just in time to save his toes.

"Oops." Lexie felt her face flame and glanced around, venturing a smile. "Well, I warned you."

"You sure did," Bob replied past the laughter.

Just then, Dominic stepped forward. "Quick—run for your lives. We have a company on the line. Save the women and children first." Then he turned toward her and grinned.

Laughter rippled through the crowd and a few people on the front did step back, but they smiled as they did it.

Playing. Dominic Santorini, the somber tycoon, was playing with her. Knowing it did something funny to her insides, made her want to steal him away and hold him prisoner so that he never lost that smile. She could drown in that smile. It was Nikos who stood in front of her, and she missed him terribly.

"Stage fright?" he asked.

Lexie shook her head, then made a production out of rubbing her hands together while she tried to still the knot in her stomach. She reached for bravado. "Okay, Bob, this time I've got it."

After Bob took his next turn, she tried again and didn't endanger anyone but missed the pole by three feet—in the opposite direction.

Bob chuckled, then took his turn again, scoring a direct hit.

"Would you like some help?" Dominic walked closer, his eyes sparkling.

It was all she could do to concentrate. She shook her head. "Not on your life, buddy. This next one will hit, you'll see." She ignored the skeptical looks around her and forced herself to focus, shutting out everyone around her.

She threw and barely breathed as the curved iron arced through the air—

And clanged around the pole, swirling until it hit the sand.

"Yes!" Lexie leaped up, throwing her fist in the air.

Dominic caught her around the waist and swung her in the air as the people around them cheered.

Between them, all went silent and breathless. Lexie lost herself in his ebony gaze, feeling him all along the front of her, his body against hers sending shivers over her skin.

Then he blinked, and the noise around them crowded in. Suddenly, Lexie remembered that they were surrounded by at least fifty people. She stepped away, rubbing her hands against her shorts to keep from reaching for him.

Dominic saw the moment she fell back to earth and cursed silently that he was the boss, that all these people looked up to him. That he had no idea who this woman really was or if he could trust her.

And just as the glow of her green eyes began to fade, he let impulse take him. Today would be a day out of time, time out of mind, a vacation from reality. It was a picnic, an occasion for levity. He would seize it and wring it dry of all its promise.

"Come with me," he urged. *Let tomorrow take care of tomorrow. I'll be Dominic Santorini tomorrow. For the rest of today, I want to be Nikos.* Only a man. A man who wanted this woman more than his next breath.

He could see the doubt in her eyes. "Just to wander," he soothed. "Simply to enjoy the moment."

"But you're—"

He shook his head. "I'll be no one. No corporation, no gala, no employee, no boss. No A. Grayson, no Dominic Santorini. Just a man and a woman."

He could see temptation battle with fear. He even thought he saw guilt, and he damned it. *I don't want to know*, he thought. *Not today.*

"How are you at volleyball?" he asked.

Her eyebrows rose. "I may be short, but I'm feisty."

"Spirit can move mountains." Dominic grinned and held out his hand. "This way, hotshot."

When she placed her hand in his, he closed his eyes for one quick moment. *Just today,* he pleaded with the fates. *Just this little while. Then I'll be responsible again. I'll remember my place, my duties.*

Lexie pulled on his hand and skipped ahead. "Hurry—time's a-wastin'."

And for one brief moment, he felt lighter and younger than he had in years.

Lexie kicked off her huaraches and stood on the edge of the sand.

"Everyone, this is Lexie Grayson," Dominic said. "Where do you want us?"

"You serve, B.D. We could use a break," one woman said.

He pointed to the center of the middle row. "Lexie, how about there?"

She took her place, then turned to look. Those strong muscular legs were spread as he prepared to serve the ball. Hair disordered by the wind, he flashed the pirate's grin and something in those dark eyes reached out to—

She turned away quickly. Oh, God. Her goose was cooked. He looked like seven kinds of sin, and Lexie knew she was doomed. Just behind and to her right, she could feel him. *Feel* him. His touch. His gaze. Could remember the body beneath those clothes. She should never have agreed to this.

His serve rocketed over the net. No one could return it.

Was there anything the man didn't do well?

Settle down and pay attention. She focused forward, trying to forget who was behind her. Then the ball headed her way, and she was forced to move fast. She was so rattled that her return landed right in the net.

"I'm sorry," she said to the rest of the team.

The guy next to her shrugged. "No sweat, babe. You just stand there and look good, and we'll watch the ball."

"I think I'd look better standing over there under the trees."

One woman laughed. The guy flashed her a grin. "I'm Gary."

"Lexie."

"Where do you work, Lexie?"

"I'm designing the set for the gala."

"No sh—no lie? I hear it's really gonna be something."

"I hope so. I'm trying my best."

"So, you married?"

Lexie laughed in surprise. "You don't waste any time, do you?"

"Ms. Grayson is not married," Dominic intervened. "She is, however, a member of this team, as are you. Would you care to ask any other questions before we continue?"

Gary shrugged and grinned before stepping back into his spot. "Hey, B.D. Can you blame me for checking her out?"

Lexie flushed to the roots of her hair. Glancing around at smiling faces, she finally dared a glance at Dominic, only to discover he had moved closer, his dark eyes intense upon her despite the humor in his voice.

"Perhaps, like a good schoolmaster, I should remove you from temptation. Why don't you serve?" Dominic handed the ball over and took Gary's place beside Lexie.

"The view's pretty great from back here, too," the cocky voice answered.

Lexie was constantly amazed at how different Dominic was with the people who worked for him. There was nothing of the unapproachable stranger. The respect and affection he engendered was constant and impressive. The people of Poseidon worked hard, but they worked as a team.

"Serve the ball, Gary."

"Party pooper."

Lexie laughed, and Dominic's head swiveled her way. The look in his eyes stole her breath.

She jerked her gaze away and concentrated on the game.

The action was fast and furious—and fun. Lexie began to see that part of what made Poseidon great was its people, their dedication to excellence, whatever they did. They played as hard as they worked.

Her hands stung from the impact of the ball, but she was getting better. She'd missed too many, but Dominic was always there to cover. Their team was ahead until Bradley joined the other side.

He glared across the net at her, and she wanted to take a step backward from his displeasure, wondering what she'd done to earn it.

He served the ball as hard as Dominic, and it rocketed straight toward her. She knew she could never return it, but her feet wouldn't seem to move.

Dominic threw himself in front of her just in time, spiking the ball so it could be returned, but because Lexie hadn't moved, he unbalanced her, and they both fell to the sand.

Dominic rolled quickly to take the brunt of his weight from her and pulled her close.

Time froze as she lay half sprawled across his

hard body, every cell in her wanting to inch closer, to plaster herself against him.

She jerked up, but his hand at her back held her captive for a second, plenty long enough to feel his body's reaction to their nearness.

The heat of the day, the fire of his touch... Lexie felt dizzy, dry of mouth, unable to breathe. Unable to think, as those dark eyes held her in thrall.

"You all right, Lexie?" someone asked.

The team crowded around them, and Lexie sprang to her feet. "I'm fine." Her vision grayed and she swayed slightly.

Dominic steadied her. "Come with me," he commanded. "You have been out in the heat too long." He pulled her off the sand and reached as though to pick her up. She took an awkward step to the side.

He looked at her oddly, then dropped his hands. "Please. Sit under the tree. I will bring you water." All playfulness had vanished; his voice turned formal again.

"I'll be fine—" But she was talking to his back.

Lexie walked to the shade, sank to the grass and dropped her head to her bent knees. Oh, God. She was in trouble.

In just moments she felt him even before she heard him approach.

"Here. Drink this. I have also brought a damp cloth."

It would be cowardly to remain curled up against her legs, right? But oh, how she wanted to hide.

Almost as much as she wanted to be near him.

Oh, Max, she thought. *I don't want to believe Dominic knew.*

She felt a cool dampness slide over the nape of her neck and shivered. Her nipples rose, her every sense aware of his nearness.

"Lexie, drink this. Please."

Though it went against every grain of sense, she lifted her head to find his own very near, his breath whispering across her cheek.

Ebony eyes studied her, troubled and weary. He was so alone, even in the midst of this crowd of people who admired him so.

His head moved toward hers a fraction, and she stopped breathing. Stopped thinking, caught in a moment of exquisite longing for a state of grace she'd experienced only once.

In this man's arms.

Her eyelids began a slow descent as his mouth neared hers.

"Oh, Lexie, are you all right?" Mrs. Murray rushed toward them.

Lexie jerked back. Dominic straightened, cursing beneath his breath.

"Oh—I—" Mrs. Murray halted, glancing back and forth between them. "Perhaps I should—"

Dominic handed Lexie the glass, his face a stone mask of reserve. "It's all right, Mrs. Murray. If you would care to sit with her a moment, I will see to a few details."

Without a glance backward, he walked away, his long strides putting distance between them.

"Oh, dear. I'm sorry, Lexie. I didn't realize—"

Lexie squeezed the older woman's hand, still shaken by how close she'd come to casting away every concern but how badly she'd wanted him to kiss her. "It's fine. Dominic was only being a good host."

Mrs. Murray, ever the soul of discretion, didn't argue. But her eyes betrayed her doubts.

Dominic made it halfway across the recreation area, cursing himself soundly, before he noticed where he was. He stopped, hands on hips, and exhaled a great gust.

So much for his holiday from reality. If Mrs. Murray hadn't come up, he'd have had Lexie on the ground beneath him, lost in his rage to protect her, to seal her, to mark her as his.

Damn Gary for noticing that tempting backside. Damn Bradley for playing rough. Damn every man here for wanting her. She was his.

But she could not be. Not until he could prove her innocence. He was not so lost in lust that he couldn't see the danger of trusting the wrong person. The wrong woman. It was an early lesson he'd taken too long to master.

He wanted to smash something with his fist. He wanted to fight, to rail against the fates that dropped such a woman in his life at the very worst time—

and made it impossible for him to know whether to trust his heart or his mind.

Then he heard her laughter. And sighed. What would it take to free him from the spell she'd woven?

What would it take to wipe her out of his mind?

Six days. In six days, the gala. In seven days, he could have her out of his life. He wouldn't have to see her every day, have to hear the laughter she gave to everyone but him. Wouldn't have the constant reminder in the smiles she left behind on the faces of everyone she met.

Then he could concentrate. He could redouble his efforts to eliminate the threat to Poseidon. He could give his sister more attention when his own wasn't so frayed.

Seven days.

A lifetime. And at the end, what would he have?

His life back, an orderly, controlled life. Not a tomboy in sight.

Damn it.

The laughter rang out again and he followed its music. Lexie rode the carousel, a dark-haired toddler in her lap. She sat the wooden horse easily, smiling at the child whose relaxed posture indicated total trust.

She would be an incredible mother. Dominic could so easily picture the nursery Lexie would create, a magical kingdom to make a child as imaginative as she was. The small dark head nestled between her breasts, and Dominic was seized by a powerful image—his own dark-haired child, carried in that woman's body.

He went hard in a rush. Even more dangerously, longing swept through him like a storm. She could be a traitor, he reminded himself. A spy. There was nothing sensible he could do but wait.

And try to stop wanting her.

Chapter Seven

He could be a thief, Lexie thought as she glimpsed Dominic a while later, surrounded by employees all vying for the attention of the man responsible for this Utopia of a company. Women preened for him here much as society ladies had done at the Starlight Ball. Men respected him, admired him, sought out his counsel. Was he a charlatan, a powermonger, or the man who'd wiped grease from her cheek?

She itched to confront him, to get it all out in the open.

Don't you dare jeopardize your contract with them, trying to be my champion. But Max didn't understand how badly she needed to know. Lexie

was caught between loyalties, between her dearest
friend and the man she could not seem to forget.
She wanted choices she didn't have.

She entered the ladies' room in search of a faucet,
as much to cool the cauldron of her mind as to
splash her sun-warmed skin. When she entered, she
heard voices and readied herself to be friendly when
all she really wanted was refuge.

Then the words sank in, hasty whispers.

"I'm telling you that Mr. Stafford blew up at one
of the temps over nothing at all, and even B.D. is
looking worried. My friend Janine in accounting
says there's a problem, that the company's in trouble."

"Poseidon is steady as a rock, girl. What kind of
foolishness you listenin' to?"

"My husband and I just bought our first house. If
I lose my job—"

"Get on with you—that ain't gonna happen. Anyway, Legend Quest is coming out real soon, and we
gonna be rollin' in the bonus money. I hear it's the
hottest thing ever to see the market."

"Then tell me why B.D. told us to double-check
every badge, every day. Something's wrong, I'm
telling you. I've never seen him so worried."

"B.D. ain't never let us down before, and he ain't
gonna do it now. You just ain't been here long
enough, girl. I been here practically since the beginning. This company been through rough times be-

fore. B.D. don't get scared. He pulled rabbits outta the hat before, he can do it again.''

''I hope you're right.''

''Why do you think everybody believes that man walks on water? 'Cause he always comes through.''

Lexie heard the stall doors open and quickly shuffled back to the outside door, her mind whirling.

Poseidon was in trouble?

She didn't need anyone to tell her that the devotion of Dominic's employees was returned full measure by the man they called The Big Dog. Hadn't she watched him all day, surrounded by people who acted as though he was the Second Coming? She'd watched him accept their regard with serious deliberation. No puffed chest for him, no monster ego, just a quiet acceptance of his role as the pillar on which the phenomenal success of this company rested.

If the company were in trouble…if the success of Legend Quest were that important…

How far would Dominic Santorini go to safeguard the well-being of all these people?

Lexie sank back against the wall. Here, at last, was a reason she could believe. She'd fought the image of Dominic, even cold as he'd seemed, being a man who would pay any price for ambition. Oh, he was ambitious, all right—no one who wasn't could have created the powerhouse that was Poseidon from out of nothing.

She'd read up on him since they'd met and knew

the story now—how he'd started with only the money from selling his car—and his formidable intellect and will. He'd gathered a group of people together and kept them all going on a shoestring budget, literally working out of the garage below his tiny apartment.

With a combination of killer hours and fierce determination, he'd created a company that now employed several hundred people, with millions of dollars in sales worldwide. And he'd done it and still commanded the affection of his employees, who seemed to be his extended family.

So if his back was to the wall and all that was threatened, how far would he go to protect them? It made an awful kind of sense, eased her mind a little that she had not been so wrong about the nature of the man who had stolen his way inside her heart on that magical night.

But it didn't excuse what had been done to her dearest friend. And she still didn't know what to do.

Perhaps it was time to go. The party was far from over, but her time had run out, she thought. Head whirling, she began to work her way through the crowds, trying to find the path to the parking lot.

She passed through a grove of trees, wondering what had attracted the crowd she could see gathered in the open area past the horseshoe pit. As people moved, she caught a glimpse of two figures in some sort of combat.

A fight? Surely not. Everyone at Poseidon seemed

to get along so well. She shook her head and kept going, but when she reached the right flank of the group, she glanced over and stopped in shock.

Dominic was one of the figures. Lean runner's legs, strong bare feet, arms flexing with ropy muscle, he towered over Josh Logan.

And aimed a kick at the boy's head.

Lexie gasped, then realized he didn't make contact.

She frowned and moved closer, trying to understand what was going on. "What is this?" she whispered to her nearest neighbor.

"B.D. is teaching Josh martial arts."

"He knows martial arts?"

"Oh yeah, honey. You should see B.D. and Mr. Stafford go at each other in the gym. They've been training together for years. Both are real gung-ho about it—that's how he gets all those muscles, that and running every day."

She watched Dominic stand next to Josh, murmuring in low tones, one hand on the boy's shoulder. Josh's adoration shone clearly in his gaze. Then Dominic turned and saw her. For a second he hesitated, an odd look on his face, his gaze seeming to bore right through her.

Then Josh looked over and spotted her. He waved, a self-conscious grin on his face. "Mr. Santorini, he's showing me how to defend myself."

She resisted the urge to shrink back into the crowd. "That's good. What are you learning?"

Josh's face lit. "Want to join us?"

Lexie stepped back. "Oh, I don't think I—" Around them, people began to clap and urge her forward.

"Come on, Ms. Grayson. It's not hard—well, not the first part, anyway."

She hazarded a glance at Dominic. He gave nothing away, his usual mask firmly in place.

"Come on, I'll show you what I just learned." Josh moved closer. "See, hold your arms like this." He demonstrated. "Now come at me and try to hit me in the chest."

"Josh, I can't hit you." Lexie didn't think she'd ever hit another person in her life. "I don't like fighting."

"This isn't fighting, Ms. Grayson. This is self-defense."

"I don't care. I'll take my chances at talking my way out of trouble." She grinned, backing up another step.

She came up against a hard chest and jerked as though she'd touched a hot stove. Whirling, she realized that Dominic had moved behind her.

Ebony eyes she'd never forget seemed to see down into her soul. "Sometimes one has no choice. Talking is not always an option." He moved a step closer, his very presence making the air around them shimmer with heat and memory. "Allow me to show you a few basic moves."

"I'm sorry. I don't think so." She'd never

minded the limelight but right now she was painfully aware of all the eyes upon them. "I'm just not the physical type."

Dark eyes raked her, and she might as well have been naked. "I beg to differ."

She backed up a step. "Why don't you two just go on? I'll just play like I'm a girl and watch, all right?"

The people around them chuckled.

"I thought you did not like being treated differently because you're a woman."

In the midnight depths, she saw a pirate. Remembered a hot Sunday afternoon.

A hotter Sunday night.

Lexie swallowed hard. "Depends on who's doing the treating," she answered tartly, rewarded by another round of laughter.

Dominic studied her for a moment, and suddenly she was back in her swinging bed, feeling his hard, powerful body, knowing his exquisite touch. Swept away on a tide of rapture so intense she could barely breathe.

He broke off the glance and turned to Josh.

Released from the spell, Lexie's knees turned to mush.

"Remember, Josh," he said, but he looked back at her. "Do the unexpected. If your opponent expects resistance, do the opposite." He held up one hand, closed into a fist, then released it. "Give way. Melt, do not force." Grip, relax. Grip. Relax. "It will upset your opponent's balance and give you the advantage.''

''Yes, sir,'' Josh replied, but Lexie was left trying to figure out if there was a message there for her.

He was never what she expected.

Dominic turned away and focused on the boy, ignoring her completely as he continued to demonstrate.

Lexie took his advice. She melted. Into the crowd, away from his very disturbing presence.

As she neared the pavilion, she heard the music. Normally Lexie loved to dance, but right now, dancing was the furthest thing from her mind.

''Hey, Lexie, come join us. Know how to line dance?'' Bob's eyes sparkled.

She shook her head. ''I'm not really into country music.''

''You like to dance, though, right? Girl with your bubble's got to love to dance.''

Lexie shrugged slightly. ''Usually, but maybe not tonight. I think I'd better go.''

His eyes rounded in horror. ''You can't leave this early—the party's just getting started. Come on, just one dance, okay? If an old geezer like me can learn to do it, a pretty young thing like you surely can.'' He leaned over and whispered like a conspirator, ''Besides, rumor has it they're doing the Chicken Dance next.''

''No way.'' Lexie had heard about the Chicken Dance from a friend with roots in the German communities surrounding Austin, but she'd never seen it.

Bob lifted his hands. "Would I lie to my new friend? Come on, Lexie, live a little."

And behind his carefree manner, she saw the widower trying to learn to live again. Knowing herself for a soft touch, she relented. "All right. One dance."

"One dance *and* the Chicken Dance."

She grinned. "It's a deal."

Dominic did not dance. He could, and often would, when necessity called, but he barely remembered a time when he had danced for sheer pleasure—

As Lexie danced now.

And Dominic watched, unable to keep his eyes from her.

Watching was enough. Almost enough.

Not nearly enough.

Her flame-bright hair bounced as she laughed and half stumbled through the first awkward steps of the Chicken Dance, an exercise in self-abandon surely hatched by a mischievous mind. Totally devoid of self-consciousness, arms akimbo to mimic flapping wings, Lexie stuck her tongue out one side of her mouth as she concentrated on her feet. Her natural grace asserted itself quickly, missteps concerning her not in the least.

She was too busy laughing, green eyes alight, face

flushed with a pleasure she showered on everyone fortunate enough to be around her.

Or even to be watching.

She was a flame in the darkness, the light that guided a weary traveler home to safety and comfort and refuge.

He wanted her so badly he ached. Literally. Like a man in the grips of ague.

When the dance ended, the entire assembly applauded. Lexie glanced around, startled when she realized it was for her. Cheeks aflame, she grinned and sketched an exaggerated bow.

The band segued into a slow song, and before logic could stop him, Dominic let longing lead him to her.

She was surrounded by a crowd, but as though an invisible thread linked them, she looked up as he approached. The group around her gave way, and Dominic held out his hand.

Not a word was said. Words were barriers; he wanted touch. He had to touch her, had to warm himself at her fire. So despite the confusion circling in her gaze, battering at the walls he'd erected between what was smart and what he needed, Dominic led Lexie onto the dance floor and pulled her into his arms.

He heard the hitch in her breath. "Dominic…"

"Sh-hh—" He wanted to be Nikos again, for just a moment. He wanted to go back to a night when they had been more than two strangers, less than reality...when they had found something together that he'd searched for all his life.

Please, Lexie, he pleaded silently. *Let us be who we were, not who we really are. Just for now. Just for this dance.*

And as if she'd heard him, Lexie sighed softly and settled against him.

He felt her over every inch of his body. His hand tightened at her waist as his insides began to hum like the electric singing of a high-tension wire. She made his every cell vibrate with a gut-deep need for her, yet a strange sort of peace settled around his heart, as though her mere touch was the oasis he'd been seeking without ever knowing he was lost in the desert and dying of thirst.

In an act as foolish as it was essential, Dominic consigned his doubts about her role in his current troubles to another place, another moment.

For this one moment, this one dance, he was Nikos and she was Lexie, and that was all either had to know. He pressed his lips to her hair and pressed her against him, knowing that she would feel his body's reaction.

She pressed her cheek against his chest and nestled closer, the movement of her flesh against his wrenching a not-quite-stifled groan from deep inside him.

Lexie felt the vibration, registered the squeeze of his big hand swallowing hers, bringing it close between them. His fingers brushed the top of her breast, and a sharp hunger clawed its way down her whole body.

It was the most delicious kind of torture to be here in public, surrounded by others, unable to move as she wanted, say what she wished…yet locked inside a space so intimate they could have been alone. Should have been alone.

Oh, how she wished for an escape to a world where only she and Nikos existed. For that's how it felt, as though she had Nikos back. She could smell him, could feel him, could see him if she'd open her eyes—

But instead she squeezed her eyes shut, trapping the moment behind them, keeping reality at bay for just a little longer. She didn't want to think about all that divided them, all the repercussions of forgetting who he was, what he'd done.

Maybe…

Stop it, Lexie. Aren't you almost sure you saw the proof with your own eyes?

She hadn't realized how she'd tensed until she felt his hand slide up and down her back, soothing her, urging her to settle against him once more. He pressed another kiss to her hair, and her heart ached with longing.

Lexie lifted her head, wishing she could find the truth, find a way out, find some solution that would work for them both—

She realized suddenly that Dominic had worked them out of the center and into the shadows away from the crowd. Eyes so dark she could drown in them pulled her in, drew her like magnets. She tilted her head, entranced, watching his head lower to hers, feeling his breath brush her cheek, wanting to know again the power of his kiss—

The music stopped, and Nikos—

No, not Nikos. *Dominic.* A man she didn't know, a powerful man who was all but a stranger.

But she knew her own willingness to let that pass, to ignore the lessons of her past, her mother's warnings. *Look what happened to me. Never let a man sweep you off your feet.*

What did she really know about him? her mind cried out, overruling her longing, a need so deep and brutal that she knew to her marrow that it could destroy her.

Hadn't the past taught her more than enough about the price of needing too much? Hadn't she failed, again and again, at being the kind of woman a man really loves?

He wasn't offering to love her, and love was what she must have.

He was Dominic Santorini, not Nikos, and if she let herself love him, she would be lost.

With sudden, stark terror grinding deep into her bones, Lexie jerked out of his arms—

And ran from the sheltering trees, from the temptation of his body, stumbling as tears blinded her eyes, escaping the mistake she wanted so badly to make, despite all reason, all powers of logic, all the memories that didn't seem to make one bit of difference to her foolish dreamer's heart.

Dominic started after her, heedless of the stares, determined only to find her, to bring her back, to make her—

A jerk on his arm whirled him around. Bradley's eyes shot sparks at him. "What the hell do you think you're doing?"

"Not now." Dominic turned, eyes searching for Lexie, but she'd vanished.

Bradley stepped in front of him, blocking his path.

Every fiber of Dominic's body itched to shove his friend aside.

"Stop it, Dominic. Have you lost your mind?"

"It's none of your business."

"The hell it's not. Poseidon is mine, too."

Dominic shot a furious glance at the man who stood in his way. "Poseidon is mine, more than anyone's."

Bradley's jaw worked. His voice was tight. "You didn't build it by yourself, and I refuse to let you do something so stupid. Do I need to remind you of Celia?"

The barb hit its mark. Stung. "Lexie is not Celia."

"You don't know that."

"She couldn't—she would not do such a thing."

"You didn't think Celia would, either."

Fury grayed his vision, but no amount of fury could change the fact that Bradley was right. He hadn't seen Celia's perfidy until it was too late. It had taken a very long time to recover from that mistake, from realizing that the woman he'd planned to marry was working with a competitor, sharing information gleaned from Dominic's pillow talk. He'd been in love, he'd thought; Celia had been, like so many others, in it for the money. Yet even knowing he'd been so wrong about Celia did not change how he wanted Lexie now. His palms itched with the need to hold her, to make them one—

In the white heat of passion, all logic flew out the door.

And that very thought sobered him, cooled him down. No woman had ever gotten to him as Lexie had. Stubbornly, he clung to what he wanted to believe. "She is not involved."

"And just how do you know that?"

"In here." He tapped his chest. "In here, I believe that."

He could not blame his friend for the derision that sprung into his eyes. He would have done the same if Bradley had said something so foolish.

Dominic settled his hands on his hips and exhaled in one powerful gust, his eyes cast to the ground. "I want to believe it."

"Dominic—" But his friend's voice was more gentle now.

He had to remember that Bradley had been his

closest friend for years. He had known Lexie for only a matter of days.

Dominic cursed beneath his breath. What had gotten into him? How had he let one small woman get to him like this? He swallowed hard and lifted his gaze to his friend's. "I apologize. I was out of line."

Bradley was still frowning, but the strain in his face eased. "Women." He tried for a grin.

Dominic could not join him.

"Look, so we don't know anything for sure. We'll give her the benefit of the doubt." But his tone made it clear that he had none. "Just promise me this, Dominic. Promise me you won't ask her directly. Don't give Kassaros a chance to have an inside line to our thinking. Please—promise me that much."

Dominic studied his friend, his mind working furiously. He would pay careful attention, even more careful than before, to her every movement. But he would watch everyone more carefully and hope that someone would slip up, that the true insider would be revealed. He cursed the need for such discretion, but it was paramount that word not get out to the markets that they had problems, not when stock was riding high on anticipation of Legend Quest.

He would find the proof he needed to clear her. Legend Quest would debut, they would restore their cash flow, and he would buy back all the stock he could find so that they were never vulnerable again.

He would prove Lexie innocent, make the company whole, take care of those who depended on him, and then, when all was secure—

He would make Lexie his, would take them back to the night of magic again and again.

But if he told her that she was under suspicion, the tiny tendrils between them would be crushed beneath that weight. She need never know. Bradley's suggestion was right, for many reasons.

"All right." He nodded. "I will not speak of it to her."

Bradley's whole frame relaxed. "Good." He glanced around them. "You want a beer or something?"

Dominic turned and watched all the people dancing and laughing and could not imagine rejoining them. He felt as if he'd been run through a wringer. "No. What I want is for this to be over. All of it."

His friend nodded sympathetically and clapped him on the shoulder. "I hear you. Why don't you go on home and I'll play host until the end?"

Dominic wanted to take Bradley up on his offer, but it was his company, his duty. He shook his head and reached for a smile that didn't come easily. "Thank you, but no. Perhaps a beer would be good."

With only one glance back in the direction Lexie had fled, Dominic followed Bradley back into the fold.

Lexie sat on the porch in an old lounge chair, her dry eyes examining every line of the swinging bed.

She'd come out here as soon as she got home from the picnic, hoping for surcease from the pain of the memories filling every cubic inch of her home.

She clutched Rosebud to her so tightly, the patient cat squirmed. Where could she get away from the memories? How could she evade the pain?

She was so confused. Her pirate Nikos was gone, vanished like the mist of morning. Burned away by the sun of a powerful, successful man. Dominic Santorini had no need of a silly dreamer who lived in her imagination more often than the real world.

Despite the miracles of that one night, she was still skinny little Lexie Grayson whom men found so easy to leave. She'd seen Dominic's type of woman at the ball, in the newspaper clippings. Never in a million years could she be tall, sleek and glamorous. She might not be such a misfit anymore, might have learned to be comfortable with who she was, might be proud of what she'd built. She might have even gotten prettier.

But deep inside, where it counted, she was still skinny Lexie Grayson, who drove a pickup and lived in a dome.

Lexie Grayson, who'd made a big mistake, who'd led with her heart and just had to get over it. Because the basic facts couldn't be changed.

"He robbed Max, Rosebud," she murmured, rubbing her cheek on the cat's head, suddenly cold in the warm, sultry night. "Maybe he didn't do it himself—I can't bear to believe that. But he had to know about it, had to approve it, and he hurt my best friend.''

She stirred in the comfortable chair, pulling the cat closer. She curled up against the pain. ''But, Rosebud, no matter what else...I miss my pirate Nikos.'' The tears from her eyes plopped softly on the gray cat's head.

There would be no sleep tonight, she could already tell.

But thank heavens, there was always work.

Tenderly, she placed the cat on the cushion and headed for her purse. The warehouse would be nice and quiet and if she were careful, she wouldn't wake Max, who lived upstairs.

And maybe, just maybe while she was working, she'd figure out how to tell him that she'd made love with the man who'd stolen his dream.

Dominic woke up with a start. His dream had been so vivid; a breathtaking interlude with Lexie in a room filled with candles. He'd made love to her slowly and with achingly sweet care. He'd heard her sighs and caught them with his kisses.

He'd felt her delicate hands all over his body, marking him forever with her passage. He'd soaked up the raw hunger of her passion and his own, delving into the secret, tender hollows of her body as if diving for treasure.

He'd felt warm and cherished in a way he'd never

known before he'd met Lexie. The warmth of her
smile, the delight in her eyes…the heart-stopping
magic when her body touched his…

Then a chill had crept over them, and shards of
desperation marred her green eyes. He'd seen a
shadow darken them, snuffing out the reflection of
warm candlelight. He'd felt her pulled out of his
arms and known his enemy possessed her. He'd felt
his heart rend as the darkness moved within him. As
knowledge of perfidy filled him, the sorrow in her
eyes chilled his soul.

As Peter Kassaros walked away with his love,
Dominic Santorini knew he'd been betrayed once
again. The rage and the pain searing through him
eclipsed his previous anguish by a factor of
thousands.

He wanted to talk to her. He had to know she was
all right. Needed to know what to believe about
her—and about himself.

He didn't feel as if he fit inside his own skin
anymore. Who was he, the man who'd laughed and
loved with Lexie in blissful ignorance—or the man
who'd built an empire and encased his heart in lead?

Dominic's cold eyes narrowed; Nikos's hand hovered over the phone.

And in the deserted dome, there was only a cat
to hear the phone ringing.

Chapter Eight

Lexie stood on a scaffold, examining the skeleton of the giant golden figure that would be the centerpiece of the inner chamber of Legend Quest. She realized she'd been staring at the same arm joint for a long while, wondering what mattered. Wishing she could walk away from this job.

You're not a quitter, Lexie. Oh, but she wanted to be. This time, just this once, she wanted to be a quitter very, very badly.

She was still shaken to the core by the day just passed. Seeing Dominic, watching him with others…hearing about the company troubles…being in his arms again. That she still wanted him so badly, despite the evidence of wrongdoing, rocked the very foundation of who she thought she was.

"Lexie? What the hell are you doing here at this hour?"

She turned too quickly at the sound of Max's sleepy voice and lost her balance.

"Watch out!"

She grabbed the scaffolding, twelve feet up in the air. Her heart sped up, adrenaline surged.

Max was already starting to climb toward her.

"I'm okay, I'm okay. Stop hovering, Max. I'm not going to break," she huffed.

"You're going to break your damn neck if you don't stop mooning over someone who doesn't deserve you," he snapped.

"I'm not mooning."

"Then what are you doing here at three in the morning, staring off into space like a lovesick calf?"

"I don't want to talk about it," she growled.

"You're hurting. Tell me what's wrong."

She was so tired she could barely see straight, so confused she couldn't think. "I can't talk to you about this. Just leave me alone. I'll figure it out."

"You've always talked to me about everything. Why not now?"

She couldn't meet his gaze.

His eyes narrowed. "Lex, why do I think there's more to this than some guy and a one-night stand?"

"Don't call it that."

He grabbed her arms and lifted her off the scaffolding. "There is more. Explain."

"Set me down."

"So you can run away? Not hardly."

She stared past him and sighed, then looked back at him. "What's happening with your search for a lawyer to help you force Poseidon's hand?"

His brows drew together. "Nothing. I have no proof, and no reputable firm is going to tackle Goliath when this David doesn't even own a slingshot. And stop changing the subject."

"What kind of proof do you need?"

His eyes narrowed again. "Don't even think about it."

Too late, she wanted to say. Would a lawyer listen if she said she thought she'd seen his Easter egg on Josh's computer?

The part of her that clung to the hope of Dominic's innocence didn't want to say more, but Max had been her best friend for so long...

She had to find out for sure first.

She had to talk to Josh again.

"Lex—" Max ran his fingers through his disordered hair. "Go home. Get some sleep. Do your job at Poseidon. I'll be fine." He shrugged as if it didn't matter. "I'm already working on a new program. This time I'm working on a computer that doesn't even have a modem. Everything will be fine, you'll see." He slung one arm around her shoulders. "Stop trying to take care of everyone you meet, kid. Just go knock 'em dead at Poseidon and don't worry about me.''

Oh, Max... If only it were that easy.

Lexie walked back from the design team's office, heading toward the lobby of Poseidon with a heavy tread and a headache the size of North America. She wished at this moment that she'd never spoken to Josh, never heard the details he'd given her.

"Hey there, Lexie. You're at it early," her friend Bob said.

She shrugged, tried for a cheer she couldn't feel. "Early bird gets the worm, my mother always said."

"If you're into worms, that's a good thing. Me, I only like them for fishing."

Her laugh didn't come easily. She hoped Bob couldn't hear the difference. Her sleepless night— and her conversation with Josh—had taken a toll. She'd never felt more torn in her life.

Max needed her help, no matter what he might say. He'd never get justice without proof, and she was in a position to give him what he needed. She could tell him that she was almost certain she'd seen his Easter egg on Josh's computer, and now she knew that Josh had written a program to break passwords. He could take that to a lawyer who could then file to stop Poseidon from launching Legend Quest.

And Bob and all the people she'd met at the picnic would be hurt. Their livelihoods would be threatened, if the gossip she'd heard had any merit, if Poseidon was really in trouble. She felt like the serpent in the garden.

"You find Josh okay?" His attention was diverted. He smiled. "Hi there, B.D."

Lexie's fingers dug into her purse strap. Her heart set up a triphammer beat.

"Good morning, Bob," said a deep voice that haunted her dreams. "Good morning, Ms. Grayson."

"Hello." She swallowed hard, wishing she could vanish. She forced herself to turn.

Oh, God. He was at his most intimidating, dressed in a killer double-breasted suit, his shirt blinding-white, his tie neatly knotted.

"Board meeting this morning, right?" Bob asked.

Dominic nodded but didn't take his gaze off hers. "Yes. Big day."

He was the very image of power, of command. Remote, intimidating in that dark, dangerous way of his. He inhabited a world she couldn't imagine, looked capable of anything, including stealing Max's creation.

Gone was the laughing dark gaze, the easy, long-limbed grace of her buccaneer. This man radiated undeniable power, was clothed in the robes of a world that was light-years from her own. This man had sophisticated women at his beck and call, jetted all over the world, had built an empire.

Now, more than ever, she felt the enormity of the chasm between them.

What would a man like him need from someone like her? The answer was simple: nothing.

If only her heart would listen. If only she could forget his touch, if her eyes would stop drinking in the sight of him.

If only his dark eyes didn't look so troubled.

"Ms. Grayson, may I speak with you a moment?"

Lexie took an involuntary step back, fingers clutched tightly around the strap of her portfolio. "I, uh—don't you have a meeting?"

Midnight eyes bored into hers. "Not for an hour. Please—this will only take a moment."

She felt Bob's gaze switching between them. "I really need to go. Could this wait? I could—I'll—" *Stop stammering, Lexie.* But she was only too aware of where she'd been, what she'd been doing. She sucked in a deep breath. "I have another appointment. I'll call Mrs. Murray."

"This will only take a moment, and I'm afraid it cannot wait." The command was unmistakable; her options limited.

Her guilt transparent?

"All right. Five minutes is all I can spare, I'm afraid."

The remote, hard stranger nodded curtly. "This way, please." He led the way into the elevator.

Silently she followed, trying to breathe over the

pounding of her heart. After last night's near-miss, she didn't trust herself alone with him.

When the doors closed, the air pressed in upon her, the atmosphere crackling with the tension between them. Lexie looked straight ahead, seeing in the shiny doors the reflection of the forbidding stranger at her side.

The image put everything into perspective. He dwarfed her, so tall, so strong, so perfectly groomed in dark, somber shades. She wore bright leggings, long dangling earrings and a tie-dyed top.

She wanted to run, far and fast, and never see him again.

She wanted him to touch her so badly she ached.

"I—I really don't have time to go all the way up to your office. Can—could you tell me what it is right here?"

For a moment the air sizzled with her daring, with his dark, piercing stare.

Then he leaned forward and hit the stop button.

And turned to her, his eyes blazing.

She took an involuntary step backward, only to feel her back against the wall. Every nerve in her body leaped to alert, knowing before her mind could register exactly what he intended.

Wanting it more than her next breath.

For a moment he looked as though he might say something. Explain, ask questions, demand answers. All of that and more shot like sparks from those fathomless dark eyes.

Then he cursed beneath his breath and closed the distance between them, the heat of his body rolling over her in waves, slamming into the blaze roaring inside her.

"Nikos—" she begged. But she didn't know if she was begging him to stop or to do what her torn-to-pieces heart so badly wanted. "We can't—"

He ignored her completely. His mouth covered hers, smothering her words as he pressed the lean muscled length of him against her. His kiss became her whole world, his body her only reality, her need the only question, his touch the only answer.

Oh, God. Lexie sobbed into his kiss, dropping her portfolio and purse and sliding her arms around his neck, pressing herself into him as though he could keep her from flying off the earth.

"Mr. Santorini?" The intercom in the elevator crackled. "Something wrong?"

Dominic's fingers dug into her back, pinning her against him.

Lexie jerked away, shattered by the knowledge of what she'd almost done.

What she still wanted to do, despite all reason, all sense.

He stared at her for a moment that spun out for what seemed eons, his eyes a maelstrom of hunger and need—and loathing.

Self-loathing rose to choke her.

"B.D.? Do you need help?"

He shook himself as if awakening from a dream.

"No." His voice grated. "We are fine." He hit the button again, and the elevator began to move.

"You're sure?"

Dominic's voice hardened as he stared at Lexie for a moment longer, shaking his head but responding in the affirmative. "Yes. I am sure."

The elevator stopped on his floor.

Lexie gathered her things, held them against her like armor. She couldn't meet his gaze again. "I— I really have to go."

He gathered up his own belongings. His voice was not quite steady when he spoke. "We need to talk."

The door opened, and Lexie was keenly conscious of the receptionist staring their way. "I don't think that's a very good idea." She couldn't imagine that he couldn't hear her heart pounding out of her chest at her daring.

She pushed the button for the lobby, wishing she could vanish.

He held the door with one strong hand and turned toward her. "We will talk." His voice was hard now and so remote.

She risked a glance. "I have a lot of work to do to be ready for the gala."

His dark eyes blazed. "If you value your contract, call Mrs. Murray today. You pick the time, but it must be today." He looked as though he wanted to say more, but already, people were heading toward him, demanding his attention.

"I don't think I'll have time—"

"Today, Lexie." He took his hand off the door, and it began to close. "Or I will come after you."

Her protest was swallowed up as the doors slid shut; the elevator began its descent.

Lexie's legs buckled and only the wall behind her stopped her from sliding to the floor.

Chapter Nine

Dominic should have been pleased as he emerged from the day-long board meeting. He'd obtained consent of the full group to implement the poison pill whenever he thought it necessary.

It should work. As soon as whoever was acquiring the stock reached sixteen percent, it would trigger a Securities and Exchange Commission disclosure. If he set up a management contract with an exorbitant buyout in case of a takeover, it would discourage such an action, too big a hit on earnings.

If he put the poison pill in place right now, the threat would disappear. Just like the Hydra of mythical lore, however, it would crop up elsewhere—if the enemy's name was Peter Kassaros.

If he lived a hundred years, he didn't think it would be long enough to understand why Peter had hated him all of his life. When they were children in Greece, he'd thought it was simple childhood rivalry, bully against a weaker child.

Perhaps he should have left it there. Dominic hadn't consciously set out to humiliate the bigger, older Peter. His fierce pride, however, wouldn't let him knuckle under. Never telling anyone else about the petty tortures and the sadistic pleasure Peter took in his games only added fuel to the fire, it seemed.

Coming to this country hadn't changed a thing. Peter had followed.

Dominic's success had made it worse.

But Peter's treatment of Ariana had upped the ante to a new level. Dominic had to stop him, had to find a way to neutralize the threat forever. Had to find out who Peter had put inside his organization.

Even if it was Lexie.

Lexie. God. He squeezed his eyes shut and rubbed the bridge of his nose, wondering what in the hell had possessed him to lose control this morning.

But he knew. It was the guilt in her eyes that had undone him. Her guilt bashing against what he knew was right…and what he wanted so badly he could taste it.

He wanted to know that Lexie was innocent. He wanted her in his arms, in his life, and he wanted it with a hunger that was eating him alive.

But he could not forget what he'd heard from the security guard this morning.

Lexie had been to visit Josh again. Why?

"Dominic, wait up," Bradley called.

Yanked out of his dark thoughts, Dominic hadn't quite erased the frown from his face before turning to face Bradley.

"What's the matter? I don't understand why you didn't let the board go ahead and enact the poison pill. Are you sure you know what you're doing?"

Dominic's words came out more clipped and hostile than he'd intended. "Yes. I do." He turned back to head toward his office, then stopped and hung his head briefly, blowing out a breath. He waited for Bradley to catch up.

"Sorry," Dominic said, sparing his friend a glance. "Not your fault. I am just so damned tired of this."

"So why are you waiting? You could have checkmated him in there just now and removed the threat." He studied Dominic's face in challenge. "But you didn't. Why?"

Because then whoever it was would back off. And he'd never know if Lexie—

He shook his head. "We don't know it's Peter yet," Dominic reminded him in a neutral tone.

"The hell we don't," Bradley countered. "You feel it in your gut, just like I do. So what's the real reason?"

Dominic remained silent.

Bradley's eyes narrowed. "It's her, isn't it?"

Dominic knew better than to ask who Bradley meant.

"Goddamn it, Dominic, what the hell are you doing? Do you know she was with Josh this morning?"

"Yes," Dominic snapped. "I know that."

"And what are you going to do about it?" Bradley's nostrils flared. "I'll tell you what I'm going to do—I'm going to see Josh and find out why. I don't know what it takes to make you see the truth about that woman, but if you won't act, I will—"

"No."

"What do you mean, no?" Bradley leaned close to him. "I've never seen you like this, not in all the years I've known you. The company is in trouble, and you're letting her lead you around by the—"

Dominic held himself back with extreme effort, reminding himself of all the years this man and he had been friends. "I will take care of it, Bradley. I will talk to Josh. You stay out of it."

Triumph flared in his friend's gaze. "When?"

"Don't push it. This is my company, and I know my duty."

"It's not just your company, my friend, or have you forgotten?"

He'd never wanted more to smash his fist into someone's face, and the very thought rocked him. What was it about her that could make him hesitate to act, make him want to take out his anger on his best friend?

With an effort like none he'd ever exerted in his life, Dominic forced his savage urge back under iron control. "I said I will take care of it. Now if you'll excuse me—" He turned and walked away before he did something he would regret forever.

"You're losing it, Dominic," Bradley stormed before he turned. "No piece of tail is worth it."

Dominic gripped the handle of his office door so tightly his knuckles turned white. With extreme care, he closed the wooden slab between himself and the only man he truly trusted.

Inside his office, Dominic shed his suit coat and loosened his tie, running a hand through his hair, wondering what the hell had happened to him.

He stared out his window across the hills, in the direction where Lexie's dome lay. It already seemed years ago that he'd been there.

Where had she been in the early dawn hours? Why hadn't she answered the phone?

And what was she doing, talking to Josh?

He shook his head as his thoughts whirled, none of them pleasant. Too many questions, not enough answers.

"Mrs. Murray," he spoke into the intercom. "What time is my appointment with Ms. Grayson?"

"I beg your pardon? Was I supposed to make an appointment for you?"

"She hasn't called." His jaw ground.

"No, sir. Would you like me to call her?"

"No. I will take care of it." He'd like to head out there right now and track her down. Have it out and get his answers, for once and for all.

But would she tell him the truth?

And did he want to hear it?

Dominic ran his fingers through his hair again, then straightened and punched the intercom again. "Mrs. Murray, please check to see if Josh Logan is in the building."

"You *what?*" Max bellowed. He reached her in one step and whirled her around by the shoulders. He closed his eyes and took a deep breath, obviously struggling for composure. "Say that again. No—" He held up a hand. "On second thought, don't say it. I don't want to hear it." Wheeling away, he paced rapidly. "I don't want to hear that my best friend— my *idiot* friend, I might add—is so foolish, so careless of her own welfare, so certain that I can't take care of myself—" He stopped and glared at her. "You lied to me, Lex. You risked— Damn, do you realize what could happen to you? Industrial espionage is no laughing matter. I could wring your neck—"

He started pacing again.

"I just wanted to help you, Max. You've worked so hard to make your dreams come true. Your work has been stolen, and you said yourself that you had to have proof for anyone to take you seriously—"

"And you just happened to be there, anyway, so—" He swore darkly. "Lexie, this is serious—it's not a game of cloak and dagger."

"I know that—" She burst into tears.

He stopped immediately and rushed to her side. "Oh, kid, I'm not—it's just that you scare the hell out of me sometimes. You're loyal to a fault and you're so impulsive." He rested his cheek on her hair and rocked her slowly as she sobbed. "Hey…it's not the end of the world."

Her heart was breaking into a million pieces. "It's worse than you know, Max."

He leaned back. "Why?"

Here it came. She had to tell him, and how much could even Max forgive? But she was so confused, so torn, she didn't know what was right anymore.

Through the blur of her tears, she tried to focus on her oldest friend. "Do you remember the guy—" Her voice dropped to a shamed whisper. "That guy? That night?"

His brows drew together. "What guy?" Then understanding dawned. "You mean, the one who—the one who got to you?"

She nodded, then dropped her gaze to the floor. "I don't know how to tell you this, Max."

"I'm your friend, Lex. Nothing can change that."

How she wished it were true. "It was Dominic Santorini."

Max's breath whooshed out in a gust. "Holy—"

"I'm sorry. I'm so sorry—I didn't know—I didn't

know who he was until—'' She lifted her shoulders, determined to face him. "Oh, Max, I—''

"Good God.'' Max paced, his face shell-shocked. She felt an inch high.

Then he whirled. "You poor kid.'' His blue eyes filled with sympathy.

"You're not mad?''

"Lex, you're my best friend. You wouldn't—'' He broke off as it hit him again. *"Mama mia.* What a mess.''

"I don't know what to do. I can't believe the man I—'' Looking around and finding no tissues, she wiped at her nose with the back of her hand. "I can't believe he'd do that, Max, but I saw your Easter egg on Josh's computer and I—''

"Whoa, whoa. Wait a minute.'' Max glanced around, then seized a rag and thrust it into her hands. Lexie blew her nose and tried not to wish she were dead.

Max sucked in a deep breath, then pulled her over to a nearby platform. He stalked toward the refrigerator and came back with two soft drinks, holding one out to her. He dropped down on the plywood beside her.

"All right.'' He shook his head, then reached out and hugged her. "We'll figure this out. Just tell me what's happened—and don't leave out a thing.''

Lexie sucked in a ragged breath and began talking.

* * *

Dominic walked back into his office at the end of a very long day and sank into his chair, staring off into the darkness, wishing he had never spoken with Josh.

The boy had confirmed Bradley's darker suspicions. Lexie had been talking to him about hacking into computers and, like the callow youth he was, Josh had never stopped to question why.

Never mind that he'd admitted to creating a program to break passwords. Didn't the boy understand the implications of that? He damn sure hadn't thought about the liability for Dominic or Poseidon if it was ever used to steal anything from another computer system.

He was only fifteen. Just a kid. Brilliant—and naive. Josh was Bradley's find, his shining star. Bradley would be furious, feeling about Lexie as he did, to know that Josh had what appeared to be a major crush on her.

How would she react if Dominic confronted her about her visits with Josh, if he asked her intentions?

The Lexie he'd met that one magic day seemed so ingenuous, barely more sophisticated than Josh.

But the Lexie whose gaze was filled with guilt? The Lexie whose unease around him led to questions?

There were so many questions Dominic wanted to have answered. If he'd never known Celia, he would have just asked them. But once a man learns that he can't trust his heart, he gets a little gun-shy of asking what's in another's.

Did he really want to know if Lexie had come after the Poseidon job by accident or by design? Was Bradley right that his desire for her was clouding his mind? Could he live with himself if he found out she'd duped him?

Could he live with himself if he didn't know?

He cursed, long and low, and buried his face in his hands. He stayed there for a moment, fighting for air.

Then he lifted his head and stared at his reflection in the dark glass.

You've never been a coward before, Nikos. Go ask her.

The turbulence in the air reflected that in Lexie's heart. A cold front was on its way south, but for now, the humidity hung like damp laundry. Since she loved to watch a storm build, Lexie had opened the doors of the dome, leaving only the screen doors between herself and the outdoors. In deference to the heat, she'd stripped to her silk chemise, which barely brushed the tops of her thighs.

She prowled the interior, Rosebud cuddled in her arms. As she scratched the cat's jaw, Lexie tried to cope with Josh's revelations, with Max's confirmation that the innocent Josh's decoding program could have been used by anyone—including Dominic.

And what of Dominic? Even if she could prove that he didn't know, the fact remained that she'd spied on him, plain and simple. How would he stomach that?

And what about that kiss? What about the hunger, the insane desire to forget everything she'd learned, to ignore everything but how something in him called to something deep inside her? Even now, knowing what she did, knowing how easy she was to dupe, she could not find it in herself to care.

Could not forget him.

Ragged from lack of sleep, raw from the unabated hunger she felt for one man, nerves frayed by turmoil, Lexie was desperate to escape.

"Music, Rosebud. We need music." She looked over her selections. She considered soothing, then rejected the idea. No classical, no Sade. Maybe bluesy ballads, Teddy Pendergrass, Luther Vandross. No. Her mood matched the weather—edgy and turbulent.

Melissa Etheridge. Soon the raw, smoky sounds of Melissa's voice filled the dome with sensuous, poignant, aching need.

"Come on, Rosie. I'm too raw to eat, and sleep is out of the question. Let's dance, girly cat. Let's just dance." She began to move around the room, losing herself in the painful glory of someone else's desperate longing. She hoped it was a hell of a storm tonight.

* * *

Dominic threw down his book in disgust. He'd read the same sentence five times.

He stared out toward the Austin skyline, the distant lightning matching his mood.

Finally, his jaw tight, he shoved his feet into deck shoes and stalked to the garage, climbing into his Jaguar, burning rubber as he left.

He placed a call from his cell phone to Mrs. Garcia, asking her to tell Ariana that he didn't know when he'd be back but not to worry. He gripped the steering wheel tightly, the jagged edge of hunger gnawing at his insides as he wished the miles away.

It took two wrong turns for him to finally find the right road. When he turned down the driveway leading to the dome, he wondered if she'd hear his engine and run out the back to escape him.

As he stopped, he glanced up at the building thunderheads. A blue norther headed this way. The weather suited his disposition: full of heat and turbulence. Charged. Crackling. Unpredictable.

When he stepped out of the car, he knew his worries about her hearing amounted to nothing. Her sound system was cranked up to a level that probably meant she'd heard nothing at all. He stopped for a moment to identify the sound.

Melissa Etheridge…hot and sensuous music. Perfect.

He couldn't stand still a moment longer. Ready or not, he had to see Lexie.

Had to touch Lexie.

He walked to the open door. And stopped dead in his tracks to watch her.

Like a kick in the gut, looking at her hit him hard. Dancing with the cat, head thrown back, long, slender throat arched and exposed, clad only in deep violet curve-hugging silk.

Watching those hands stroke Rosebud's fur and remembering them on his own skin…seeing her eyes closed, her hips swaying…he itched to touch her. Craving rocketed through him—no slow syrupy desire, but raw, jagged desperation.

He opened the screen door and stepped inside.

She sensed his presence and whirled to face him.

The storm's energy intensified as lightning cracked the night. Thunder rumbled in the distance.

Lexie clasped the cat before her like armor. Her eyes widened, her pupils grew huge as she saw him standing in her doorway. She didn't speak.

Her longings came to life before her, as if conjured up by a voodoo priestess. Sweat dampened his T-shirt, revealing the curves of every muscle she couldn't see. Her gaze caressed the bronzed hardness where she could. Razors of desire sliced, treacherous and deep, as she imagined licking up each rivulet of salty promise.

Dominic's nostrils flared as her scent drifted to him on the quickening breeze. His gaze devoured the gentle swell of her breasts as lace curved to barely cover her nipples, plunging into the sweet valley between and disappearing behind the cover of the cat held in front of her like a shield.

She was going to need better protection than a cat.

He stepped forward, propelled by raw hunger too long denied. Driven by dreams of rapture. Heated to a burning pitch by the ache of trying to deny what was real.

He was real. She was real. They were here, together, on this storm-tossed night. He would sort it all out later. For now, he had to touch her or lose his mind.

He stalked her like the predator he was.

"Nikos—Dominic..." She held up her hand as if that would stop him.

"Nikos," he rumbled, stepping closer.

She skirted a chair, placing it between them. "We have to talk."

"Not now." He moved toward her again, sure steps leading him to what he now knew was inevitable.

If Lexie didn't understand that, he would show her.

She stepped away again. Rosebud yowled.

"Put the cat down, Lexie. She can tell what's going to happen, even if you are too stubborn to admit it."

Her nostrils flared. Her eyes sparked in temper.

He found himself smiling.

"I don't know you, Nikos. I don't know who you are."

"No words, Lexie. Not now. Words are the enemy." He reached out, sliding his fingers into her hair as he pulled her close. "Touch me. We will talk, but right now I have to touch you." He lowered his head, his breath whispering across her lips. "Let me back into the magic, Lexie. Forget everything but who we were that night."

His eyes darkened with pain and longing and hunger. With every fiber in her being, she wanted that, too, wanted to go back to the magic.

But Max... "Nikos, I can't—" Her voice trailed to a whisper as she studied him.

He looked so tired, so careworn. The wolf standing outside the fire, hungry and alone. She thought of all of the people who depended on him. Her own doubts crowded in, the sense she'd had from the first that he was special, that he could be the one—

"I need you, Lexie." Exhaustion colored his voice and she realized that even this indomitable man could be vulnerable, that the lone wolf needed rest, needed solace.

Nothing could have moved her more. Again her instinct that he knew nothing of the theft reared its head. The man in front of her was not a thief—in her heart she knew that as deeply as she'd known anything. And she'd told Max what she knew. Max himself had told her not to take this on her shoulders any longer, that he would go forward now.

This man's touch mesmerized her, sent slow, sweet, molasses-thick longing swirling through her veins. She needed him, too.

He brushed her lips, murmuring something in a mixture of languages, something raspy and impossibly erotic.

When she opened herself to him, winding her arms around his neck, he groaned his hunger and despair.

As he drew her sweetness into him and drank from the clear waters of her crystalline spirit, he pulled her against him, wrapping his arms tightly, wanting to absorb her.

He lifted his mouth just a fraction. "I am starving. Let me have you." He growled a warning. "Hold back nothing. I want it all."

The dam burst within her. Rushing waters of desire surged and overran all her reasons, all her questions. She let need deluge her, drench her, pressing her body so closely she could feel his sweat soaking into her skin. With what small movement he allowed her, she brushed her breasts along the hard wall of his muscled chest.

He responded as if she'd jolted him with a live wire, moving his mouth away from hers to torture hot kisses over every inch of her skin. His wicked tongue teased and tormented, his long, gifted fingers bedeviled and seduced.

Not close enough, Dominic anguished. *I cannot get close enough.* His hands slid over the smooth curve of her hip, cradling her sassy behind as he pulled her against him, aroused to a fever of jagged, piercing need.

Greedy, yet dying to make it last, he gritted his teeth and sucked in air in a desperate bid for control. He pulled his hands away for a shuddering, dangerous moment and struggled to slow down.

"Lexie...I need you too much." He had to touch her...had to. He took one finger of each hand and slid them under the straps of her chemise, clenching the muscles of his abdomen against the ragged edges of a composure fraying worse with every moment that passed. As he slid the straps off her shoulders, he placed a gentle kiss where each one had touched her delicate skin.

Lexie was having none of his self-denial. She all but crawled over him inch by inch, her nails digging into his skin as she responded to the depth of his hunger.

Dominic gave up all pretense of restraint. He devoured her mouth with his own, while he scooped her up in his arms, never breaking the kiss. He tore himself away for one desperate moment and growled, "Which bed?"

With no hesitation, she chose the one that would bring them closer to the storm. They would be surrounded by an energy field almost as strong as the one that crackled and flashed between them.

"Outside."

He grinned, the slash of white teeth brilliant

against his bronzed skin. "Ah, Lexie, you'd make a good pirate yourself." He covered the ground quickly, coming to a halt out on the porch, where they contemplated the majesty of the thundering sky.

But not for long.

No longer trying to fight their deepest longings incited hearts with desire too long suppressed. Fears of the future added fuel to the intensity of the flames.

Lexie's skin rippled with goose bumps as the quickening breeze stirred. She released herself to the man she craved, letting his kisses follow the wind as it caressed her body.

Gently, ever so gently, he laid her on the swinging bed, slowly rocking it as he stood beside it, knowing his heart was in his eyes. Her own generous heart spoke as she opened her arms to pull him down. Lexie poured a tender oil upon the raw edges of his mind, soothing and healing the pain that had not ceased since he'd left here so few days, yet eons ago.

As he dragged the silk down her body, he covered each inch with cherishing kisses, as if in prayer and blessing. He'd never felt such raw need...ached with such tenderness. He filled his hands with her flesh; he stroked her satin skin, soothed and aroused with his tongue. But over it all, beyond anything he'd experienced, the night glistened with something stronger, richer. Something he didn't dare name.

Lexie's skin burned, it thrilled, it wept at his touch. His hot tongue, his silken kisses, the whisper of the wind as it skimmed her flesh, all galvanized her, sent her soaring to another realm. The storm within her matched the building fury of the storm outside—and Nikos was the sorcerer, calling fire from the sky. His strong hands spread her open, ranged over her as his fingers traced her hidden folds, sliding within her deepest secrets. When he lowered his head, licks of fire danced over her nerves. When she felt the first sultry touch against her most sensitive flesh, she writhed in a longing so strong it was painful.

''Nikos…Nikos…'' Her head rocked from side to side as the bed rocked beneath her. She lost her bearings in the unspeakable bliss, the needles of her compass confused by the storm. Dizzying rapture overcame her, exquisite ripples of pleasure sluicing over nerve endings aroused beyond bearing. Without the will to resist, she followed her pirate to ecstasy.

Dark satisfaction filled Dominic as he watched her fly on the wings of delight. It was almost enough to give this to her. He could almost ignore the inferno inside him—somehow giving to her had become more important than satisfying himself.

Until she opened her eyes and the heat of her gaze

pulled him down to burn with her, turn to ashes in the red-hot blaze. She tore at his clothing in urgent demand, sliding her hands slowly up his chest as she pulled off his shirt. Her fingers stroked along the waistband of his shorts, and he gasped as she wrapped those delicate fingers around him. She pulled him down on the bed, then moved to reverse their positions.

"It's been too long since my hands have been here," she teased, eliciting a groan of pain and pleasure. She grazed her nails lightly over his body, with lazy, catlike clawing. He sucked in a harsh breath of violent need.

"Lexie..." He couldn't find the words.

She arched a flirting eyebrow, slicking her tongue over her lush lips, then trailed one long, sizzling wet path down his belly, one torturous dip into his navel. As she nipped with her teeth, she soothed with her tongue, all the time letting her nails torment and delight. When she encircled his shaft with her lips and caressed the full sensitive weight beneath, his hips moved of their own accord, all sense of control lost.

She looked like a warrior princess, the storm-clouds building behind her. Lightning exploded at her back as she drew him into her spell.

He stood it as long as he could, the vicious torment. When she threw her head back and laughed in delight at his growl, he grasped her waist and lifted her, groaning at the prospect of filling her. She stopped, perhaps as galvanized by the sensation as he was. He couldn't help what he said next.

"Home...this is home, Lexie."

Her eyes filled with tears as she nodded. Her lips trembled as she placed a finger on his. He sucked gently upon that long, delicate finger for an endless moment too precious to last.

Then the fever claimed them.

He reversed their positions and towered over her, holding her face in his hands as he possessed her. He held her gaze with his own as he let go of the last remnants of logic, knowing only that he was crazed to have her, that the roaring in his head obscured all reason.

All he could see was her, all he could feel. In a deep growl he warned her, "I want it all, everything you have. Do you understand? Everything, Lexie."

She lifted trembling hands to stroke his brow, and Dominic knew then that he would consign the rest of his life to the flames of hell to keep her, if that's what it took. A savage need to make her his own rose within him. He pulled her close but never let his gaze leave hers as he reached deep within his own heart to find the man worthy of this woman's generous spirit.

The heavens crashed around them, and he drove within her like a man possessed.

Lexie gripped him tightly, wrapping those long legs around his waist as she feasted greedily on his mouth. The sky lit up with flares of lightning; the thunder matched the roaring of their blood.

She sobbed as she shattered; he poured himself into her, crying out her name. As Lexie and Dominic found their way back to their own private paradise, the heavens opened up.

And the healing rain began to fall.

Chapter Ten

Her head pillowed on his chest, Lexie slept cuddled against him. Outside, the fierce storm had blown itself out, a gentle, steady rain falling, the air blessedly cool for the first time in months.

The breeze whispered across the patio. Goose bumps rose on her skin, and he tugged her closer, rolling them to cover her with his body to keep her warm. He pressed a kiss to her hair, his heart too full. He ached. He wanted. Reason and regret danced a ragged two-step and wouldn't be brushed aside.

He shouldn't have come. She was everything he'd remembered—and more. Both generous and greedy,

she'd responded to his touch as though she were
made only for him, fervent with a need that matched
his own as if she felt the same desperation to return
to the bliss they'd once shared—

Before it was lost to them forever.

Desperation. Guilt. Longing. They had been there
in the green eyes, in the clutch of fingers, in the
depths of her kiss.

He didn't want to know.

But he had no choice.

Dominic wanted nothing more than to lock them
both away forever in Lexie's magical kingdom, the
only place he'd ever found peace.

But duty called.

Beneath him, she stirred and sighed softly. His
body leaped in answer. Casting away reality for another moment, he bent his head to nuzzle her throat,
smiling against the hum of her pleasure.

"Mmm..." She sighed again, one graceful arm
stretching above her head.

He lifted his head, greeted by sparkling green
eyes. Gently, almost reverently, he brushed a kiss
over her lips. "Good morning."

She smiled, and it was like the sun breaking out.
"Good morning."

Then the phone rang.

Lexie groaned. Dominic cursed. "Leave it."

She smiled. "Okay." Slender fingers slid into his
hair—

Then she went stiff at the sound of a voice on her

recorder. "Max—" She sat up quickly. "Something sounds wrong." She turned to him. "I'm sorry, I have to—"

Dominic rolled over and let her go, silently cursing Max to perdition while willing his unruly body to behave. He studied her delectable bare backside as she answered the phone, smiling as she groped for a throw on the sofa and wrapped it around her.

He wanted to see every inch of her sweet flesh, damn it. He stood and strode toward her, determined to do his part to get her off the phone.

Then he saw her eyes flash in alarm as he approached, saw guilt flare as she turned hastily and lowered her voice to a whisper. Heard the name Josh.

And reality slugged him right in the jaw. Max? Her friend was in it with her? What the hell was going on?

He whirled and headed back to the porch, jerking on his pants. One glance at the bed and a million images rose up to taunt him, memories so sweet and hot they smote him right in the heart.

His promise to Bradley be damned. He was going to clear this up right now. He could not wait another minute. No matter how he feared what he'd learn, he had to know. Now.

When he walked back inside, she'd hung up. She was making coffee, her movements jerky. When she spilled coffee grounds out of nerveless fingers, her shoulders sank as though the weight of her secrets had finally broken her. Her head dropped and he could see despair in every line of her frame.

He didn't trust his own reactions anymore. He wanted to go to her, wanted to comfort her too badly. Such a lapse was dangerous for a man such as him. He didn't have the luxury of blind faith.

He needed facts. No matter what they were.

"Lexie, are you spying on me?" There. It was out.

She turned too slowly, guilt stealing over her face, and his heart sank like a stone.

"Tell me why. What did Kassaros promise you?"

Her face was a study in confusion. "Who's Kassaros?"

Anger ran roughshod over his dread. "Don't play coy with me. What did he offer you to help him take Poseidon down?"

"What?" She shook her head as though to clear it. "What are you talking about?"

"I'm talking about the man who wants to destroy my business. The man who used Ariana—devastated her—because he hates me so much. What did he give you for spying for him? And what is Max's role in all this?"

She clutched the throw at her breasts, her brows knitted in confusion, anger stealing over her face. "You—you think I'm out to hurt your company?" Her voice sharpened. "You think—after what we—" She gestured toward the porch, toward the bed. "You think I could work to destroy your company and then *sleep* with you? That I'd sleep with you to get information?''

Waves of insult rolled off her, her green eyes sparking with outrage and despair. "How could you?'' Her voice dropped to a whisper. "If you could believe that of me, then I was more wrong than I knew. You did steal Max's software, didn't you?''

Caught up in the maelstrom of heartsick despair and roaring anger, it took a minute for him to comprehend her words. "What? What are you saying?''

"Your graphics for Legend Quest. The software to create them was stolen from Max.''

"That's impossible. The design team wrote that software.''

"No, they didn't. I saw Max's Easter egg with my own eyes, on Josh's computer.''

"No. Absolutely impossible. I would know—'' Then it hit him. "You have been spying.''

The guilt he'd seen before rippled over her features.

"Bradley was right.'' Leaden despair settled into his heart. He turned away, raked fingers through his hair.

"I had to help my friend. Poseidon is huge and powerful. He's only one man.''

All he could hear, all he could think, was that he'd been a fool. Again.

He whirled. "How long? How long have you

been spying? Do you know what can happen to you? You can go to jail for what you've done."

Green eyes sparked. "So can you. You stole Max's dream."

"Even you cannot get away with calling me a thief. I am no thief. Nothing has been stolen. You are wrong."

An odd sort of relief leaped into her gaze. "You didn't know." She closed her eyes. "Thank God. I was so afraid—"

All Dominic could think about was the devastation it would wreak on his company if she were right. She could not be right. Legend Quest was too important, the timing too tight.

And she had believed him capable of stealing from her friend. He had given her entry to his soft underbelly, to his most vulnerable self...and she thought him a thief. Could believe so little in his integrity, understand him so little.

"You could make love to me, believing I stole from your friend?" In a strange sort of way, fury receded. He grew numb. "What kind of woman are you?" he murmured almost to himself.

Lexie glanced up at him, her eyes bright with unshed tears. "A fool, apparently. You made love to me believing me a spy."

"You are a spy." His jaw tightened. It was Celia all over again. It was his greedy stepmother, saying one thing with her mouth and plotting his doom behind his back.

"I was trying to help my friend," she cried. "Max needs me."

I needed you, too, Lexie. But we were spinning in separate orbits, all along. When I thought my heart touched yours—

It had been a mirage conjured out of longings he'd thought long ago vanquished. Dominic swallowed the bitter taste of deception and headed for the rest of his clothes, pulling about him the only thing that had never let him down: the mantle of distance. It was his refuge, his reliable friend. Inside there he could function, could do what needed to be done.

The first thing was to get out of here. Get away before the acid of betrayal ate its way through.

"Nikos—"

"Do not call me that," he snapped, then brutally shoved away his fury, swallowed hard, locked it down tightly.

Then he looked at her one last time.

She looked ravaged. Vulnerable.

Dominic clamped down hard on a renegade urge to close the distance between them, to take her in his arms, to offer comfort.

Damn. What was it she did to him?

Before he could weaken, he spoke. "Your friend is wrong. I am not a thief. I do not employ thieves." He turned away, headed for the door. "Your security clearance will be revoked. Any communications you must have before the gala will be routed through

Mrs. Murray.'' He grasped the door handle in a death grip, wondering what it would take to stop this crushing ache that held his heart in a fist. How long this time to get past betrayal?

Surely this time would do it. He would never be fooled again.

Her voice came from behind him, quiet and strained but threaded with determination. ''Perhaps I don't want to do the gala anymore.''

''No.'' A quick bolt of panic skittered through him at the thought of never seeing her again. Only for the sake of the company, he assured himself. Not for him. He turned back, steeling himself to resist whatever he would see. ''You will finish your contract. To do otherwise would ruin you.''

Lexie flinched. ''Don't threaten me, Dominic.''

She should look ridiculous, standing in her kitchen, her slender feet bare, white-knuckled fingers clutched on bright woven fabric wrapped around a body he still wanted with a hunger he damned.

But she was a warrior queen, standing there, head high and defiant.

He had to get out of here before the dam broke and all the nasty jumble inside him spilled free. ''It is no threat. It is not personal, only a simple matter of business.'' He watched her wince at his cruelty. ''The gala will go on. I will investigate your claim and prove you wrong. In a few days, it will all be over.''

Those green eyes shimmered, her voice grew hoarse. "Just that simple? It's over, you walk away? That easy, Dominic?"

Why did he feel as though it was a test and he was failing?

It couldn't matter. He had made a mistake. He had a company to save. Only that could matter.

So he nodded, studiously ignoring the ache that crowded his chest, tightened his throat. "Just that simple. Goodbye, Lexie."

He walked out the door, leaving dreams and deceptions behind.

Chapter Eleven

He was gone, and he wouldn't be back. Just like her father. Just like—

Look at what happened to me, Alexandra. Never give your heart to a man. Never let him become too important.

Too late, Mama. Way too late.

Lexie stared at the door Dominic had just exited, listened to the sound of his engine dying away. Dominic—the real man. Not Nikos, the lover of her dreams.

She closed her eyes against the claws shredding her heart. How had she been such a fool? Couldn't she see? Couldn't she ever see things for what they were, not what she wanted them to be?

It was that imagination again, that stupid streak of romanticism that she just couldn't seem to stamp out.

But it had seemed so real last night, his hunger, his need for her, his tender touch. He'd taken her to heights of bliss beyond that first night's ecstasy, held her heart in his hands, stolen her breath.

Every touch had whispered of something deeper, something real and precious and fine—

And all the while, he'd known she was spying. All the while, he had made love to a woman he didn't trust. So every bit of what had seemed so real had been a lie.

And Lexie had soaked up every bit of it and asked for more. Begged for more. Given up every last shred of self-respect while moaning for more—

She had to stop thinking about it, about him. It was over. He was over. And in a few days, this job would be over.

She should call him up, tell him to go straight to hell, tell him to take his precious job and shove it. She didn't need him, didn't need his job, didn't need—

Oh, sweet mercy—even that was a lie. Lexie fought the urge to sink to the floor in despair. She did need the job. And she wanted to need him— Nikos, not Dominic. Not the cold man, not the rich man, not the powerful one.

The tender one, the laughing pirate. The lonely wolf. And despite everything she knew was smart, was sensible, a part of Lexie stubbornly clung to the belief that there had been truth between them, had been something fine and sweet and—

Pure. The laugh that tore from her throat was ragged with grief. She no longer knew the difference between truth and a lie, not if she could be this wrong.

She stared sightlessly out toward her valley, leaden despair settling around her like a shroud. She wanted nothing more right now than to sink into oblivion, to burrow away from this massive ache too huge to contain inside her chest.

Which is why she would do the opposite. She would go take her shower and wash his scent away. She would dress and she would go to his mansion and work—

Oh, God. Her knees buckled. She bent double, the pain ripping, tearing. She couldn't do this. She—

Lexie squeezed her eyes shut, gripped the edge of the counter, hunched against a hurt so big she couldn't breathe.

Have to breathe. Deep breath, Lexie. You can do this. You can't let him destroy you, can't let him win.

She sucked in one breath. Exhaled. Sucked in another.

Blew it out, exhaling the poison of betrayal.

She would work hard. Work smarter. Work as if it would save her life, her sanity, save her from losing her mind.

And she would pray her most fervent pleas that the fates would be kind, that she would not have to see Dominic Santorini until this was all over.

Straightening, forcing herself to deal with the little things first, Lexie turned and started all over to make coffee. Coffee. Shower. Work.

Not love. Never love. Not foolish dreams. Work, just work. It was pitiful protection—but it was all she had. She would make it enough, until her heart caught up.

Dominic drove straight to the office. He would use a change of clothes he kept there. By the time he had to see Ariana and Mrs. Garcia, he would have himself in hand, be back to normal.

Even as he thought the words, they mocked him. Normal would be a long time in coming. What he'd lost this morning would not release its claws until he confirmed that he was right, until he put Lexie behind him.

His hands tightened on the steering wheel as devastated green eyes rose before him. Despite all his resolve, something inside him twisted in endless, aching grief.

He didn't know what to hope for—that she was wrong, or that she was right. Either way, he lost too much.

He strode past Bob with only a nod, his mood darkening with every step. No one had yet arrived on his floor, thank God. He tore off the clothes he wanted to burn and stepped into the shower to scrub away the night.

But it wouldn't leave—she wouldn't leave him. Lexie taunted him with a thousand images, a thousand sensations, a thousand memories. And he knew a hunger so deep it gutted him.

Dominic slammed his palms against the tile and hung his head, letting the water beat down while his eyes burned as though he were a callow boy suffering his first rejection.

Why? he cried out to the fates. *Why couldn't she be who I thought she was?*

For a second he leaned back against the tile, wanting its chill to shock him back into his senses. He stared into the steam with eyes gone sightless.

No one would ever know how much he'd wanted her to be real, how much he'd needed her to be the tomboy, the one woman who wouldn't care if he had two nickels to rub together.

Dominic shook his head and took a deep breath, then shut off the shower and grabbed a towel.

"Lex, are you excited about—" Max's voice dwindled as he walked through her office door two days later. "What's wrong? What are you doing here, sitting in the dark?"

"I can't go, Max." Bright light flared as he hit the switch, and she covered her eyes.

"Bull. Of course you're—what happened to you? You look like hell."

"Thanks a lot. I didn't know you were back in town."

"I just drove in." He crossed the room and dropped to a crouch in front of her. His voice turned gentle. "Are you scared, is that it? You know the gala will turn out fine. You're a genius with the sets."

She raised her head and met his gaze. "I just don't want to go."

"You are so full of it. You love hearing people rave about your work, and this is the best you've ever—" He stopped, cocked his head. "Is this about me? Is it because of the software? 'Cause, Lex, it's going to work out. I've got a copy ordered. I'll have it tomorrow, and then I'll be able to prove it."

"It will be too late then, won't it?"

He shook his head. "Nope. Having a glitzy launch will only improve my situation. Lots of people will be paying attention, and tomorrow they'll be able to verify that it's true." He shoved to his feet, holding out a hand. "So get up and get a move on. You're not even dressed for the big shindig."

She'd brought her dress, wanting to avoid the long drive back to the dome after working all day on finishing touches. "I don't want to go."

Max stared at her for a long moment. "It's him, isn't it? Santorini. You're afraid to see him."

"I'm not afraid. He means nothing to me." *Liar, liar, pants on fire.* Despite the distance of two days, not one iota of the pain had lessened. She'd worked until she dropped and still she awakened from dreams of Dominic.

Not Dominic. Dominic lied and stole.

Nikos. It was Nikos she missed.

"Come on, Lex, spit it out. What happened?"

Max had been gone on business since that night, and she'd been relieved, having no idea what to tell him. She'd spent every waking hour at the mansion, worried sick over what she'd say to Dominic if he came near, but true to his word, he kept distance between them. She'd seen him a couple of times, but he'd acted as if she were invisible.

She had to tell Max. "Max, he knows. He says it's not true, says he'll prove it." She waited, almost hoping he'd yell at her, do something, anything, to break the ice encasing her heart. When he remained silent, she looked up. "I'm sorry. When you called before you left—" She squeezed her eyes shut, wishing she could wring out the memories of that night.

"He was there, Max. He heard me talking to you."

Max swore darkly. "What happened? Why was he—"

She shrank back into her chair, and Max cursed again. "Damn, Lexie, what were you thinking?"

She started to cry, wiping angrily at her tears. "He knew. He called me a spy. He knew I'd been spying on him and he still came to me and made me believe—" Her voice broke on a sob.

"What a goddamn mess." Max threw his arms out to the side, exhaling loudly.

"I'm sorry. I'm so sorry." She huddled in her chair, wanting to be anywhere but here, anyone but her. "I never meant—I was just trying to help—" Her voice broke.

Max began to pace, raking impatient fingers through his hair.

"Max, I don't think he knew. Dominic, I mean. He seemed truly surprised."

He turned, studied her. "So what's he doing about it?"

"I don't know. He just said he'd prove that I was wrong. He said it couldn't happen without him knowing."

Max snorted. "He may be a wizard, but he's not omnipotent." He stared at her but she could tell he was seeing something else. Then his focus snapped to her. "Get dressed."

"What?"

"I said get dressed. You're going to the gala and I'm going with you. I want to size up this guy for myself, talk to people there. The whole company will be there, right?"

She nodded.

"Then let's go." He headed for the door, then stopped and turned. "Can you handle this? Seeing him again, I mean?"

"It doesn't matter. I owe you big."

"Don't do that to yourself. You should have

stayed out of it, that much is true. But you didn't create this mess. Someone at Poseidon did. They hurt me and they hurt you.'' His voice went hard and grim. "Me, I'll recover. But no matter who's at fault over the theft, I want a piece of Santorini for what he did to you.''

She smiled sadly. "I did it to myself. I knew better. I'm just not the type men want to keep.''

"Oh, kid…'' Max slammed his palm against the door frame. "You sell yourself short. You always have.'' He shook his head. "Get dressed, Lexie,'' he said gently. "Let's go get us a pound or two of flesh.''

Dominic stood in front of the huge golden statue of Hades, shaking his head in amazement at Lexie's skill. The Chamber of Doom, the centerpiece of the game, had been reproduced so faithfully he would swear he had entered Legend Quest himself.

She was so talented. So beautiful.

Such a liar. Bradley had taken his own time late at night to vet every line of code in both the game and the software used to create the graphics. There was no Easter egg embedded anywhere within either, Bradley had told him just moments ago, taking pity on his friend and holding back the smirk he no doubt felt.

He'd warned Dominic, after all. Told him to stop thinking below his belt.

"Dominic?" Ariana's voice called from the maze outside this chamber.

"In here." He sighed, shook his head, let his dreams go. He'd never admit to anyone how much he'd hoped he'd be wrong and Lexie right, no matter what it meant to the company.

His sister walked in, a vision in a long shimmering column of pale gold.

"You look wonderful," he said.

She approached, smiling. She reached up and made a minute adjustment to the tie of his tux. "So do you." She worried at her lower lip.

"What?"

A faint frown appeared between her brows. "I'm worried about you."

"No need." He shrugged. "I'm sure the evening will go fine. If everything else is as perfect as the set, the evening will be a success."

She smiled. "Lexie did an incredible job, didn't she? The whole place takes my breath away. It's like entering another world. She's created magic, sheer magic."

She always does, he wanted to say. Beyond his command, a vision shimmered. Sky-blue ceiling, fluffy clouds, twinkling lights. A sultan's bed he would never try out.

A beautiful deceiver creating beautiful lies.

It was his own private hell that he wanted her still, wanted to be a true believer despite all that he knew.

"What is it?" Ariana asked, touching his arm. "You look so sad."

Dominic straightened, snapped out of it, remembered his duty. "Not at all. I am perfectly fine." He smiled for her benefit. "Have you seen all of it?"

"Lexie showed me this afternoon, but it looks completely different tonight. I'd love to go through it again before the first guests arrive."

"Then we shall. This way, madam." He proffered his arm and led her back to the beginning of Lexie's maze, trying very hard to concentrate on his sister and forget the woman whose memory would not leave him alone. They were almost to the front gate, torchlights flickering, the very air broadcasting menace and challenge and a sense of time beyond time—

And then he saw her.

"Lexie, this is incredible!" Ariana rushed toward her, and Lexie felt Max stir beside her just as Ariana threw her arms around her and gave a big hug. "I've never seen anything like it. It seems so real, people are going to go crazy over this, absolutely crazy. Aren't they, Dominic?"

Lexie could feel Max bristle beside her, felt the air charge with antagonism. She pulled away, looking past the taller woman's shoulder.

Ebony eyes in a buccaneer's face. His features could have been cast in stone, the torchlight flickering over the sharp angles and harsh planes. In a perfectly tailored tux, he was every woman's dream.

Her dream. Her heartache.

"I am certain they will." He looked utterly unmoved.

Her insides were quivering, and he looked as though this was just another day in the park.

Beside her, she felt Max's muscles bunch and she squeezed his arm, hoping to forestall a confrontation. She turned to Ariana, her mouth dry as dust.

Somehow she managed to speak. "Thank you. I'm glad you like it."

But the excitement had drained from Ariana's features, replaced by confusion and dread as the tension crackled around her. "Dominic?"

Instantly he turned solicitous, reaching toward his fragile sister. "It is truly a miracle. Ms. Grayson—" his voice was ice-cold and silken as he turned to her, "—would you be willing to take Ariana on a tour before things get too crowded?"

She heard the silk, but she also heard the steel beneath. Everything inside her bristled at being dismissed. "I'm afraid I don't have time right now. Max has agreed to help me do a last-minute check."

Then Max, the traitor, gave Ariana his million-watt smile. "Ariana, Lexie will worry herself to death though everything is always perfect. She does this every time. If you'd make her take you on a tour, I'm sure your brother would be grateful. Otherwise, she'll just drive all of us nuts."

Lexie shot him a glare that could have melted lead. He stared right back, his eyes fierce and determined. She glanced at Dominic. Face equally stony, he merely lifted a brow.

Ariana broke the impasse, her face brightening with compassion. "Of course. I understand perfectly. Lexie, you've worked so hard. There can't possibly be anything left to check, but I really would appreciate the grand tour."

In contrast to the despair that so often dogged her new friend, enthusiasm and interest lit Ariana's eyes. Lexie knew she would only forestall the inevitable by staying right now. Somewhere along the way, Max would confront Dominic, and neither would thank her to interfere.

It was Max's software, after all, and she had already complicated things enough. She glanced between Dominic and Max, reminded of nothing so much as two bulls about to tangle horns. The air between them literally crackled.

"I'll be glad to show you around, but I will need to be back here soon." She looked pointedly at both men. "Very soon."

"I will expect you both back in a few minutes, safe and sound," Dominic warned.

"Same here," Lexie muttered and led Ariana away.

"You bastard," Max growled.

Dominic followed Lexie with his eyes until she

disappeared around a corner. Her hair a tousled bright flame, her body caressed by black silk banded with emerald satin…the graceful curve of her throat demanded emeralds he would have gladly bought her—

If only she'd given him one gift. The gift of truth.

Icy fury slithered up his spine. "What sort of game are you playing, Lancaster? And why do you need to involve a trusting creature like Lexie?"

"Me?" Max took a step toward him, his fists curling.

Dominic would like nothing better than to relieve the pressure of the past weeks with a good fistfight. For a moment, he considered throwing caution to the winds. Bradley could host the evening while he beat the living hell out of the man who so obviously itched to plow a fist in his face.

It was one more luxury he could not enjoy. "Yes, you. What is this cock-and-bull story about an Easter egg? What is your part in all this? What did Kassaros offer you?" He took a step closer, his own fingers closing into a fist. "And how could you use Lexie like that?"

"Who the hell is Kassaros?" Max looked as confused as Lexie had.

Perhaps he was as good an actor. "Do not try to tell me that you are not involved in Peter Kassaros's bid to destroy Poseidon. You did not answer me. Why did you involve Lexie? She believes you care for her."

"I do care for her. I'm her best friend."

Unreasonable jealousy dug in spurs. "Do not confuse desire with friendship. I do not buy that. No friend would use her as you have."

Max laughed one short harsh bark. "Desire?" His eyes goggled. "Lexie? Hell, she's like a kid sister to me."

Dominic had to believe him. Truth was there in his voice. It only made things worse. "Then I do not understand how you can call yourself her friend and use her to spy for you."

Max's jaw clenched, his eyes sparking. "Use her? Hell, I ordered her to stay out of it. She's just so damn sweet and loyal. She'd fight the devil himself to defend a friend."

The devil himself. Dominic's own worth to her, summed up in a nutshell. She had not been willing to believe in him. She did not accord him even the benefits of friendship, much less give him her heart.

Dominic shook his head. "I do not understand. You did not ask her to spy. She claims not to know who Peter Kassaros is. What is going on?"

"You tell me, buddy. What the devil are you talking about?"

Dominic studied the man in front of him, uneasy about confiding his company's troubles but needing to understand where all the pieces fit. He glanced away, studying the angles. Then he took a leap as he had so often before. "Why do you believe your software was stolen?"

"It *was* stolen."

"You cannot prove that."

"Of course I can."

"There is no Easter egg."

The other man's gaze narrowed. "You may have found it and removed it from your master, but you couldn't have removed it on all those copies that will hit the street tomorrow."

"Do you have a pirated copy, is that it?"

"No. Lexie found it on the kid's computer."

"Lexie can read code?"

Max laughed. "Lexie can barely turn on her own computer. It's little better than a doorstop." Then his face darkened. "She finally paid attention for once and remembered the keystrokes I showed her to reveal it. She went into the design crew's office and tried it out, but I didn't know until days later." He muttered under his breath. "Little fool. I could have wrung her neck when she finally told me."

"My man tells me it is not there."

"Your man is lying." Max cocked his head. "You got a copy of the game here?"

Dominic nodded. "It's on my laptop."

Max gestured toward the house. "Lead the way, hotshot."

"I have guests."

"It won't take me thirty seconds. Unless you're afraid to find out..."

Dominic's mind whirled. "You do not know Peter Kassaros, you are certain?"

Max huffed out a breath. "Who is this guy you're so obsessed with? Listen, Santorini, all I want is what's mine. You don't have to show me a damn thing tonight. We can save it for the lawyers, but I promise you I will pursue you until my last breath. Those graphics were created with my program. I'd bet my soul on it."

Every line of the man's frame radiated certainty. If it were true, what did that mean? If Lexie was not spying for Kassaros, then who was?

Dominic shook his head and glanced at his watch. "I will give you five minutes."

"Like I said, big shot. Lead the way."

Lexie tried to keep her mind on Ariana, but everything within her strained to go back.

"Lexie?"

"Hmm?"

"What is everyone hiding?"

Her attention focused squarely on Dominic's sister. "I don't know what you mean," she said carefully.

Irritation snapped in the dark eyes. "Don't treat me like a child. Dominic does that already. I hate that. Stop coddling me. What's going on?"

Be careful with my sister. She is very fragile.

"I don't—"

"Ariana, what a pleasure." Bradley strode toward them, his hands held out toward Ariana.

Ariana smiled and exchanged air kisses, but Lexie

saw her subtle signs of unease. She didn't like Bradley herself, though she couldn't tell why.

Bradley was right, she heard Dominic say.

Okay, so she knew why she didn't like him.

"Hello, Bradley. Are you as thrilled as Dominic is by Lexie's masterpiece?"

Too smooth. Too urbane, he was. He made Lexie feel like a grubby urchin.

His eyes turned cool, dislike barely banked. No doubt he and Dominic had been talking. "It is indeed impressive." His voice told her he was surprised.

She lifted her chin. "Thank you. I'm delighted you approve." She didn't try very hard to mask her disdain.

His eyes narrowed. "Ariana, Dominic was looking for you a moment ago."

"But Lexie and I weren't quite finished."

"He said he needed your help."

Pride leaped into her gaze. "Really?"

Bradley smiled, but it didn't quite make it to his eyes. "Really. Go on. I need to speak with Ms. Grayson a moment."

Ariana turned to go. "Thank you, Lexie, for showing me around. It's really a marvel. You should be proud."

"Ms. Grayson has many things of which she's proud, I am sure," Bradley said, but his eyes were cold and hard and soulless, the edge in his voice grating on Lexie's nerves.

He took a step toward her, and Lexie wanted to beg Ariana to stay.

Then she got angry. This man had never been on her side. She sent the other woman a smile she didn't feel. "Thank you, Ariana."

Ariana left, and Lexie felt the atmosphere shift, a subtle sense of menace creeping in, making her skin crawl. She started to step backward, then checked herself, squaring her shoulders, lifting her chin. "Is something wrong?"

"Oh, many things are wrong, Ms. Grayson, but I intend to fix them."

He took another step toward her, and Lexie fought the urge to run.

Chapter Twelve

Dominic walked back into the madhouse, press and guests everywhere. His mind was a jumble of conflicting impulses, of questions without answers.

The Easter egg was there, exactly as Max had promised.

Why had Bradley denied it?

Shaking off his preoccupation, Dominic forced himself to murmur appropriate greetings to various guests, all the while scanning the faces, looking for Bradley.

But wishing for Lexie.

Ariana walked up, her face glowing with anticipation. "You asked for me?"

Dominic blinked. "For you?"

"Bradley told me you needed my help with something. What is it?"

He kept his voice carefully neutral. "Where is Bradley right now?"

"With Lexie in the Chamber of Doom. He needed to discuss something with her."

The back of his neck prickled. He turned toward Max. "Please—stay with Ariana." He pitched his voice low.

Max looked startled. "I was going to get Lex and take her home."

"Dominic?" Ariana's look of anticipation turned to worry. "Is something wrong?"

He smoothed his face into a careful smile, leaning down to kiss her forehead. "No. Everything is fine. Would you entertain Max for me, please?"

She glanced at Max, then back at Dominic. "Perhaps Max doesn't—"

A line appeared between Max's brows. He shot Dominic a questioning glance but then smiled for Ariana's benefit. "I always have time for a beautiful lady."

Dominic didn't spare a backward glance. He couldn't ignore the instinct that rippled up his spine, the sense that something was off. Something important. He forced himself to walk slowly until he was out of Ariana's sight—

And then he ran.

* * *

"How did you do it?" Bradley asked. "How did you turn Dominic's head? Was it the sex?" He moved closer. Though he was not as tall as Dominic, still he towered over her. "Are you that good in bed?"

"Excuse me?" She didn't try to hide her outrage. "I don't have to listen to trash like that." She turned to go.

He grabbed her arm and whirled her back to face him. "You worry me. You've got him questioning things he should be ignoring. He's looking over my shoulder, and I don't need that right now." His grip tightened painfully on her bare arm. "He will believe me, not you, when it comes down to it. I'm his best friend, his trusted lieutenant—" Something twisted in his voice, a bitter edge that didn't sound like a best friend.

He squeezed long fingers on her arm until she couldn't help crying out. "Let me go. What's wrong with you?" But his tight grip didn't relent.

Lexie began to struggle in earnest, fear an icy trickle down her back. She pulled her foot back to kick him, but he whipped her arm to the side and upset her balance. She fought to stay on her feet. "Bradley, what's wrong with you? Why are you doing this?"

"Let her go." Dominic's deep voice carried across the chamber.

Lexie wanted to sob with relief as she caught

sight of his powerful frame moving toward them. She expected Bradley to let her go—

Instead he gripped her arm more tightly, pulled her closer to him.

"I said let her go, Bradley."

The sneer on Bradley's face rearranged itself into sleek good looks again as he met Dominic's stony glare. "She's a spy and a liar, Dominic. I'm simply trying to get the truth out of her, since you won't."

"And what might that truth be?" Cold. His face was so cold, as though the answer hardly mattered.

"She lied to you, to all of us. First when she took the job, knowing she was going to use her access to spy on you for Kassaros. Then she made friends with Ariana—have you never wondered why, Dominic?"

Lexie frowned, wondering where he would lead.

"I'm sure you'll be willing to explain." Dominic's tone sounded almost bored.

"Have you thought about what would happen if someone gained control of Ariana's ten percent of the stock? You would no longer have majority control of the company."

Dominic only nodded for Bradley to continue.

"Of course Ariana would never sell to Kassaros—if she knew he was the one who wanted it. But Ariana doesn't want to live off your charity forever, Dominic. She has her pride."

"I am perfectly capable of taking care of my sister."

"But if she wants her independence? You haven't really asked her what she wants, have you? You're too busy treating her as a wounded bird."

Lexie could see that the shot hit its mark.

"What if Kassaros sent his little spy along to charm her way into Ariana's confidence, to help convince Ariana to sell her stock to some other entity as a means of obtaining her freedom?"

"She would not do that without talking to me. And I do not believe Lexie is capable of that sort of betrayal."

Lexie blinked. Even that small evidence of faith was one she wanted to grasp and hold on to.

"No?" Bradley's sneer was back. "But then, you didn't believe Celia would betray you, either, did you, my friend? I tried to warn you to watch out for her but you wanted to believe she was true to you."

A ghosting of pain drifted over Dominic's handsome features. He looked over at Lexie, and his midnight eyes studied her. "I did indeed."

She cursed the mood lighting she'd created. The sinister shadows hid too much that she wanted—needed—to see in his face. She wanted to tell Dominic that she'd never lied to him about her feelings, that he could trust the truth that blossomed between them every time they touched.

"This woman lied to you, too, from the first moment you met her. Didn't she?"

A strange look settled into Dominic's eyes. Then

he nodded. "I suppose she did." He didn't look at Bradley, only at her.

She wanted to speak, wanted to explain again.

But it was true. She had lied.

He had lied, too.

Bradley's voice held triumph. "She lied again when you confronted her, telling you that ridiculous fairy tale about the Easter egg."

"Did she?" One dark brow lifted, a spike of anger in his voice.

For a moment, Lexie dared to hope. She took in a breath to plead her case, to beg him to believe her and not Bradley, to say whatever it took to make those beloved features look at her with warmth again. With laughter and hope and longing and—

Love.

She almost groaned as the word rattled around in her brain. Was she always doomed to love men who didn't love her back? How had it happened? How had she fallen for this man whose world was too big for her, who was still too much a mystery?

But she knew. She'd fallen for the lonely wolf who needed the warmth she offered, the man who put everyone else's needs ahead of his own. The man who obviously had been betrayed before and could be forgiven for not trusting now.

"Of course she did. I told you the Easter egg doesn't exist. It was a ruse, a way to shift suspicion away from herself, to disguise her true purpose."

No— Lexie wanted to shout. *I didn't. I saw it myself. He's lying,* she wanted to say.

But a deeper realization hit her, and she subsided without a word. She would not beg, would not defend herself. The only hope for her and Dominic lay in him stepping outside his suspicion. If he could not feel, somewhere deep inside him, the truth of who she really was, then nothing else mattered. She was through begging for crumbs from men who would leave anyway.

"Is Bradley right, Lexie? Are you a sham? Is the woman I saw so briefly a mirage? Which one of you is the real Lexie?"

She swallowed hard and straightened, jerking her arm out of Bradley's grasp. "You know the truth, Dominic. Deep inside, you know—if you want to listen."

The moment zinged with tension. She felt Bradley's glare, but she only had eyes for the man in front of her, the man searching her face as though to divine her inner truth.

Then doubt rode his features, plain as day, and Lexie's hopes evaporated.

Dominic studied the green eyes he wanted so badly to believe, but doubts clamored—jeering, taunting him with the bitter dregs of memory. Bradley had been his best friend for years, his trusted right arm. He'd known this woman little more than two weeks.

He owed so much to so many. The weight of his

responsibilities demanded caution, logic, the solid ground of proof.

But deep inside him, the man named Nikos remembered laughter and ecstasy and lightness of heart. Remembered hope and joy and the tantalizing promise of a life outside the bonds that constrained him.

He'd been wrong before—desperately wrong. The longings of his heart whispered sweet nothings, tempting him away from what he knew was his duty while his reason demanded that he surrender to longing at his peril.

Lexie watched the battle raging, her hopes sinking with every moment. He would do as others had—walk away and leave her heart lying open and wounded. But this time, she wasn't so sure she could piece the battered shell together again.

Dominic's ebony eyes held hers in thrall, almost as if he were begging her to tip the balance, to give him the certainty he could not find within himself.

She couldn't do that. Wouldn't. Lexie fought the press of tears and glanced away to stop the agony of what was coming.

Then he sucked in a breath and her own stilled. "Why did you lie about the code for the Easter egg, Bradley?"

Lexie blinked in shock.

Bradley stiffened beside her. "What?" He made a rude noise of disbelief. "What lies has she told you? I'm your best friend, Dominic. We've been

through it all. Are you going to believe me—'' His
lip curled, and his glare should have withered her.
''Or a liar like her?''

Lexie glanced quickly at Dominic, surprised to
see a flicker of something warm in his gaze.

Quickly he shifted his gaze to Bradley, and his
voice hardened. ''You said you would take care of
it, you would search every line of code to be certain
that her claim could not be true. Did you? Did you
search, or did you simply tell me what you wanted
me to believe?''

''The code isn't there.'' Agitation sparked in
Bradley's frame, his voice sharp with an edge of
hurt, of insult he would not easily forgive. ''Go
ahead, if she's poisoned your mind so much that
you've forgotten how long we've been friends, what
we've meant to each other. Check my laptop. You'll
see the truth of it.'' Every inch of his body shouted
his dare.

It pained Dominic more than he would ever admit, having to press the issue. But the discrepancies
were too glaring, the stakes too high. ''I have already seen the truth. The man who wrote the software demonstrated it on my copy of the game just
a few moments ago.'' And the knowledge that his
old friend had lied was a wound Dominic would not
shrug off easily. ''Why, Bradley? What is your stake
in this?''

With a feral growl, Bradley grabbed Lexie again,
jerking him to her, wrapping one arm around her

throat, his other hand lifted in a posture Dominic couldn't fail to recognize from the many classes they'd attended, the many mock battles they'd staged, working out together. He could snap her neck in seconds—

And he looked suddenly desperate enough to do it.

Lexie choked, struggling against Bradley's hold.

"Tell her to stop moving, Dominic. You know what I can do. I promise you I will."

Dominic forced his attention away from Bradley's hands and focused on Lexie. "Be still, sweetheart. The hold he has on you is very dangerous. He could snap your neck between one breath and another." Dominic fought the talons of fear clawing their way up his throat, forced himself to keep his voice steady. "Just be very still. I'm certain Bradley will listen to reason." Though he knew nothing of the sort.

He turned to the friend he barely recognized, fury twisting Bradley's once-handsome face into a mis-shapen mask. "Let her go. She's done nothing to you."

Bradley's sharp laughter mocked him. "Of course she has—she's spoiled everything." His eyes had a far-off look, a subtle shading of something Dominic had never seen before. "I had it all in hand. I was this close, then she turned your head and upset the balance. At first she seemed a wonderful twist I could use to keep you in the dark. I'd figured a way to turn her meddling to my advantage.''

He tightened his grip on her throat, and Dominic watched fear leap into Lexie's eyes as she desperately tried to force his arm away. He took a step forward.

"Stop it—'' Bradley shouted. "Stop it or I'll get a better revenge. I'll take away something you care about even more than your precious company—'' His eyes glittered, and Dominic began to wonder if his friend was completely sane.

One wrong move…he had to stay calm, despite his savage urge to charge, to tear Bradley limb from limb. Ruthlessly he clamped down on the violence simmering inside him. "Ease up on her, Bradley. It's me you hate, not her.''

Bradley laughed, the pitch higher than normal. When he laughed, his grip eased.

Dominic watched with relief as Lexie's breathing steadied. The flush drained from her face; her skin went paper-white, her eyes huge with terror. He wished he could reassure her that he would make sure she was safe, but he didn't dare take his attention away from the man who presented a very real danger to her.

"I do hate you, you know.'' An odd peace slid over Bradley's face. "I didn't want to. It bothered me a lot, at first—because I loved you like a brother for so many years.''

He had to keep Bradley talking. Surely someone

would notice their absence. Perhaps Max would come looking. But Dominic counted on nothing except his own vigilance for Bradley's slightest mistake.

"What changed?" He couldn't quite keep the pain from his voice. "You were my brother and my best friend, the person I trusted most in the world."

"You don't have a very good track record with trust, do you, my friend? It's a flaw in your character that you want so badly to trust, yet experience should have taught you by now that it's a luxury you should not indulge."

"But we built Poseidon together. We went through so many rough times. We were partners, Bradley—partners and friends."

Bitterness echoed in Bradley's voice. "Oh, how you deceive yourself when it suits you." His face became a mask of hate. "We haven't been partners in a very long time. Everything is always about Dominic, Saint Dominic, The Big Dog, Mr. High-and-Mighty."

"You've been an important part of building this company."

Bradley snorted. "Ah yes…your trusted lieutenant, I believe *Time* magazine called me? Your indispensable right arm, as *PC* magazine stated? I'm sick of standing in your shadow, Dominic. I want to stand in the sun for a change."

"I'll buy your stock from you at a very fair price. You'll have the cash to start your own company."

Lexie could feel the tremors of fury rock Bradley's frame. His arm tightened on her throat again, and frantically she tried to slip her fingers beneath his arm to keep him from choking her again.

Dominic glanced at her, his gaze pleading. For what? What did he want?

Be still. It went against every ounce of instinct, but she forced herself to master the powerful urge to fight her way out of the hold.

She could see the tension beneath Dominic's outward calm. One hand curled into a fist, then flexed, the motion repeating.

Grip. Relax. Grip. Relax.

Bradley's laughter held only a sneer now. "But I don't want a new company, old friend. I want Poseidon."

Lexie saw disbelief slide over Dominic's face.

"What?"

"I almost had it, too." He laughed again, sharp and edgy. "You bought into the whole Kassaros scenario, hook line and sinker. Your old enemy has been a great convenience to me."

Lexie felt his arm tighten, but this time she forced herself to not tense in reaction.

Bradley continued. "I had it carefully worked out. I had to be flexible, of course. Ariana's appearance saved me the effort of having a proxy seek her out. A little wining and dining...your sister is quite delectable, Dominic. Fragile and so easily charmed by tender care—until Ms. Grayson supplanted my position as confidant.''

He leaned closer, whispering loudly in Lexie's ear. ''I really did not appreciate your very inconvenient timing. You complicated things far too much. With the new graphics software in place and clever little pointers toward Dominic, I only needed a little more time to cement my position before the launch, before he would be revealed as a thief and lose everything—but then you spoiled all my careful plans.''

She felt his other hand come up, rest against her head. A shiver ran down her backbone. She could see fear in Dominic's eyes, the knowledge that danger was only a breath away.

Grip. Relax. Grip. Relax. Relax. Re—

Suddenly, Lexie got it. His advice at the picnic—

Do the unexpected. If your opponent expects resistance, do the opposite. Give way. Melt, do not force.

Dominic's voice sounded so casual. ''How did you steal the software and integrate it without anyone suspecting?''

Bradley relaxed, boasting. ''Easier than you might like to think. Naive little Josh showed me his creation.''

Lexie stared at Dominic, who caught her look. She mimicked his hand motion, and he nodded so faintly she might have imagined it.

''The design crew had heard rumors in a chat

room from a friend of Lancaster's boasting about what he'd developed. I—''

She seized the advantage of Bradley's looser grip and let her muscles go lax, falling to the ground as dead weight—

Dominic charged, closing the distance between him and Bradley, ramming his shoulder, shoving Lexie away from danger.

She hit the ground and the breath whooshed out of her lungs. She gasped for air, scrambling to her feet, looking frantically for something to help Dominic—

But rage turned him into a man she'd never seen, a creature of immense power, of savage intent. Bradley fought back with desperation, his eyes gone feral, his lips drawn back from his teeth as though he'd gladly tear Dominic's flesh from his body. The bruises on her throat reminded her that Bradley was prepared to go all the way, that he had nothing to lose now.

She thought she heard voices, heard the sounds of footsteps, but she couldn't take her eyes off the struggle, wishing she could help.

Savage blows rained down; Bradley whirled, striking Dominic from behind. Dominic staggered, shook his head. Someone screamed, and Lexie realized it was her.

Bradley moved in, his voice shouting triumph as his hand sliced toward the tender place on Dominic's throat—

A killing blow. She watched with horror, Bradley's murderous intent plain on his face. Lexie knew a moment of fear so intense she couldn't breathe. *Nikos,* her mind cried out. *Dominic, my love—*

At the last possible moment, Dominic gave way, just as he'd instructed her. Do the unexpected.

Bradley's balance faltered. Quickly he scrambled to recover but he'd been too committed; now he was vulnerable. Dominic came at him with cold, deadly resolve, dropping him to the ground, arm raised back to strike, his face brutal as any warrior of ancient times caught in a fight to the death—

"Dominic—" she called softly, afraid to upset the balance but knowing he'd never be able to live with himself if he—

Then she saw the subtle shift in him, saw the knowledge of defeat in Bradley's face. Dominic rose, using one foot to shove Bradley to his back, his disdain and disgust complete.

She waited for Bradley to come at him again, but instead Bradley closed his eyes, threw one arm over his face.

Dominic stood over him, his expression shifting from rage to pity to pain. "You were my friend," he murmured. "I trusted you completely."

She thought she'd never seen anything more sad in her life than the anguish that passed over Dominic's face. She crossed the distance between them, wrapping her arms around his waist.

Dominic looked down at her for a moment, his eyes naked and vulnerable. Lost.

"I'm so sorry," she whispered.

A spasm passed over his features and his jaw went tight. "Do not pity me."

She lifted to her tiptoes, pressed her hand to his cheek as her lips neared his. "It's not pity, Nikos. I love you."

Midnight eyes scanned hers for truth. His arms tightened fiercely around her, his head lowering to take hers in a hot, needy kiss—

Suddenly the chamber filled with people and shouts.

"Lexie," she heard Max shout.

"Mr. Santorini—"

"Nikos—" Ariana cried.

They were swept up in the chaos. The policemen hired for security took Bradley into custody. A few straggling reporters there to cover the launch clamored for Dominic's attention. Shocked employees clustered around him, trying to understand what had happened, what it meant to Poseidon.

Dominic was swallowed up in the needs of all those people who had prior claim on him. Lexie watched from a distance, every passing moment making her more aware of the chasm between them.

It was over. Dominic was innocent, just as she'd wanted so badly to believe. He'd only had a moment to ask Max to give him a chance to discuss compensation for the theft and ask for silence until they'd spoken. Max had agreed, and Dominic was very busy at the moment making sure that Bradley's actions were explained in a way that would minimize the damage to Poseidon's reputation.

He'd asked her to wait for him, too, but she was very tempted to leave. Watching him, she'd never been more painfully aware of his stature in the world, his fame and visibility, his importance to so many people.

He was every inch Dominic Santorini, tycoon of the electronic world. Not one tiny glimpse of her devilish, breath-stealing Nikos showed from behind the reserved and serious man who stood in the spotlight of cameras and microphones only yards away.

And she was only Lexie Grayson, the skinny orphan who lived in a geodesic dome and drove a pickup. Despite the heated, hungry kiss they'd barely begun to share, she knew they were not suited. It was only the moment, the brush with danger.

She would never fit in his world, even if he wanted it. He would leave eventually, anyway. He would see it. He needed a queen, a consort who would fit by his side, represent him well. Better to walk away now, before she bled to death from a stubborn heart that insisted on wishing for things that would never work.

She slipped away, resolving to call him later and thank him. Even now, the thought that he'd believed her and not Bradley touched her deeply. She wanted to make sure he knew that what they'd had together was something she'd never forget, even as she would reassure him that she didn't expect more.

Perhaps they could be friends, though. She'd like that—

Suddenly a strong hand grabbed her arm, whirled her around—

"You said you would wait."

"Dominic, I—" Her heart sped up as ebony eyes bored into her. She glanced back toward where they'd been. "You're very busy. People need you. We can talk later—"

Dominic swore darkly, out of breath as he had not been while battling Bradley. Out of breath because he'd looked up and seen her slipping away—and known somehow that she would not be back. His voice turned harsh. "Forget what they need. What about you? What about me?"

She frowned. "What?"

He clasped her shoulders to keep her there. "You can say you love me and just walk away?"

Those green eyes shifted, glanced down. "Forget I said it. It was the heat of the moment."

His heart stuttered. "You do not mean that." His hands tightened.

Her lashes swept up, and anguish filled her gaze. "How can you tell what to believe? I have lied to you, Dominic. I spied on you. I withheld secrets you needed to know—" Suddenly her voice cracked.

"Bradley could have killed you—" Tears spilled over her lashes.

Dominic goggled. "Me? Lexie, he was within a breath of snapping your neck—to get back at me. I was not the one in danger." Until the day he died, that image would haunt him—her pale skin, her huge eyes, her slender throat beneath the hands of a man who would end her life without remorse. "I died more with every moment, watching him, knowing how easily—" His throat tightened, choking off his voice.

He pulled her into his arms, and she resisted, placing one small hand on his chest.

"Lexie, what is it?"

"Dominic, it's been a very emotional evening. We need some distance. Once you think about it, you'll see that we can't possibly—"

The edges of his vision darkened, everything around them vanishing until he could only see her, only hear in her voice that she was going to leave before they ever had a chance to begin—

"Marry me." He had to bind her to him, had to find a way to keep her. Something inside him would be lost forever if she left.

She stiffened, her head jerking up, her eyes going wide. "What did you say?"

"Don't go. Marry me, Lexie." He could see the frown begin, the tiny shake of her head. He rushed to build his case. "I will wrap you in luxury every day of your life. I will take care of you. I will show you the world, give you anything your heart desires—"

She looked at him as if he'd slapped her. "I don't need luxury, Dominic. You're talking about things. I don't care about things." Her frown deepened.

She was slipping from his grasp, and he stood there helpless to detain her.

"I love you." He'd never said those words to another soul, not since he was a small boy, easy and secure in the knowledge of his mother's love, never knowing she'd be gone before he reached his tenth birthday. His breath coming hard, he prodded. "Don't you love me? You told me you loved me. Was it a lie?"

"No." She lifted that mesmerizing green gaze to his, sadness lurking in the shadows. "I do love you, but that's not the point."

"What is the point?" He had to make her see. He fell back on logic, always his friend. "I love you. I want to take care of you. I can give you anything your heart desires."

"Stop it, Dominic." Fear rose in her eyes, fear he couldn't understand. "Let me go. Just let me go."

"I will not let you go. You are making no sense. I love you—does that mean nothing? I've never said that to a woman in my life."

She tried for a smile. "And I'm honored. But it doesn't matter."

He loosened his grip in astonishment, then

snatched her back the second she pulled away. "Stay right there. You will explain to me."

Her lips tilted upward for a fleeting moment. He found himself almost wishing she'd cry. Tears would be better than this sad certainty that filled her gaze.

"My father said he loved me every day for eight years, then one day he left without a word. I gave my virginity to a boy who said he loved me, then he walked away and married another woman." She touched his cheek gently. "Saying 'I love you' is easy, Dominic. People say it all the time. Words are easy—"

She dropped her hand. "It's staying that's hard." Her slender shoulders shrugged. "I don't know what's wrong with me that I'm so easy to leave," she murmured.

"I asked you to marry me. I want you in my life forever."

Pity. There was pity in her gaze, damn her. "Dominic, I don't fit in your world. I'm not glamorous or sleek like your other women. I'm not sophisticated or worldly." She gestured to the mansion behind him. "I don't want your money or your big house. This place is a prison."

Her chin jutted just slightly. "I like my little valley and my pickup and my dome. They're me, the real me. I could pretend to belong in your world, but it would be a sham. One day you'd regret being so impetuous."

A raw fear such as he'd never felt rippled up his spine. "Lexie, I am not being impetuous. I love you. I want to marry you. I'll stay. I will never leave you."

She closed her eyes, shaking her head slowly, a single tear leaking down her cheek. "Please, Dominic. Just let me go," she whispered.

"You're wrong, Lexie. You are exactly who I need in my life. Those sleek women meant nothing to me. I want my tomboy back. I want to see grease on your cheek. I want to try out the sultan's bed."

Her head rose quickly, a tiny spark lighting in her eyes. "You can come try it anytime you want." Her voice was fond, but still so sad. "But I can't change who I am, not even for you. The tomboy with grease on her cheek is a novelty now, but look around you—" She gestured expansively. "All those people depend on you for their livelihoods. The success of Poseidon depends on a man I don't know, a man who needs a queen by his side, not a tomboy, not a whim."

"You're not a whim, damn it. And to hell with all of them—" He reached for her, but she sidestepped him.

"Please, Dominic. Let me go. If you care about me at all, let me go." Agitation filled her slender frame. She wasn't listening to him. He couldn't reach her, and the knowledge filled his gut with ice-cold fear.

"Please, Dominic." Her voice was an anguished whisper. "I just want to go home."

Logic had failed him. Protests of love had failed him, offering marriage had failed him. How did he reach her?

He wanted to sweep her up in his arms and carry her away, hold her prisoner until he convinced her, until he made her see that her fears were nothing, that he would be there, that he would stay—

Words are easy.

Dominic looked down into the face of the woman he would love for the rest of his life and knew a moment of terrible fear that he would lose her. Knew with an inner certainty that if he pushed her now, if he forced his will on her, something infinitely precious would slip beyond his grasp forever.

Men have always found me easy to leave.

He didn't want to do as she asked, didn't want to let her out of his sight for a moment, yet as he looked at her pale face, saw the exhaustion in every line of her frame, he knew that she was beyond reasoning right now. She was not listening. She did not trust words, and words were all he had at this moment. The rest would take time.

Dominic swallowed hard and took the biggest gamble of his life. He stepped away from her, his heart tearing inside his chest. "All right, Lexie. I'll let you go home." He felt like he couldn't breathe. "But I insist on taking you there."

She glanced up at him in surprise. "You don't

have to do that.'' She nodded toward the dwindling crowd, seeing people waiting for him. ''You're needed here. You still need to talk to Max. I'll get a cab.''

He cursed beneath his breath. ''I already told Max that I would give him a job, that I want to give him a generous share of the profits on Legend Quest. Do not bother to argue. I am taking you home, and that's that.''

Then, heart aching, chest too tight to breathe, he escorted her to his car in silence, resolving that this was only temporary, that he would find a way to get through to her, to make her believe he would stay as others had not.

When they reached her dome, he escorted her inside, taking a look around to assure himself all was secure.

And then he did the hardest thing he'd ever done in his life.

He walked away and left Lexie there, alone.

But if she thought he would stay away—

She was right. She did not know Dominic Santorini.

Whose ancestors had been pirates.

Chapter Thirteen

Lexie punched down her pillow for the thousandth time that night, rolling again, searching for that elusive spot that would let her sleep—

And quit remembering.

Myriad images paraded past her closed eyelids. They wouldn't go away when she opened her eyes, either.

Midnight eyes filled with confusion, with sorrow.

Dominic watching her as Bradley imprisoned her, locking away what she now knew was fear behind the impenetrable mask.

The certainty in his voice when he said, "I love you."

The power of his kiss, the need she could taste.

Her own longing to burrow against him and never leave.

But for every image related to Dominic, others rose from her past. Her father tucking her in one night—

And gone the next morning.

Hearing from others first that her college boyfriend was getting married—to someone else.

"Stop it—" She leaped from the bed, tossed her pillow to the floor.

Rosebud yowled, darting away.

"Oh, Rosie—" Lexie sank to the floor, gathering the cat close, scalding tears leaking from her eyes.

Her arms felt empty, her chest hollow. "I'm so afraid, Rosie."

Rosebud's ears twitched, and Lexie heard it, too.

The rumble of a car engine coming up her drive.

A familiar rumble.

A T-bird.

She almost dropped the cat in her haste, scrambling from the floor, wiping her eyes as she ran to the window. She looked down in dismay at the old oversize T-shirt filled with holes.

But when she reached the window, no one was outside. Only Dominic's T-bird—

With a huge bow on its hood and sign she couldn't quite read.

She moved to the door, trying to get a good look.

She still couldn't see, so she stepped outside, glancing around to be sure no one could see her.

He'd vanished—or someone had. Or they were hiding, but whatever the explanation, she could not stand it—she had to see.

Lexie tiptoed over the damp grass to the T-bird, peering at the tag tied to the enormous bow—Free To A Good Home—With One Condition.

Lexie frowned slightly and looked around for the owner.

Dominic emerged from a clump of trees, his hands up in surrender, his smile that of Nikos, not the very serious owner of Poseidon.

He looked so good he stole her breath. Made her ache. Black T-shirt, black jeans…he looked every inch the rebel, the marauder.

"All right. I give up." But mischief danced in his gaze.

The hard knot in her chest loosened slightly. "Give up what?"

"I won't ask you to believe in my words. I won't tell you I love you or ask you to marry me again. I want a simple business arrangement. We can put it in writing."

Lexie frowned. "What kind of business arrangement?"

"You once told me my car needed a better mechanic, did you not?"

She cocked her head, wondering where he was headed. "I did say that."

"Do you see anyone here you might suggest?"

Lexie leaned forward. "You want me to be your mechanic?" It was a long way from being a wife.

He might keep a very straight face, but his eyes were dancing. "The sign says free to a good home—" He gestured around them. "Is this a good home?"

"Dominic, you can't just give me your car."

He folded his arms over his very broad chest. "I can do whatever I want." One eyebrow lifted, and he'd never looked more like a pirate. "You will recall, however, that there is a condition."

"A catch." She muttered. "I knew it. You shark business types always have a catch."

He laughed, and she wanted to press her mouth to his strong, tanned throat. Wanted her hands on him so badly she could barely breathe.

"Yes, Ms. Grayson, one might call it a catch."

She couldn't fight her grin. "What kind of catch?"

"There is no better mechanic for this magnificent vehicle than myself—no disrespect intended." White teeth flashed in a thoroughly disreputable grin. "I could not let it go to a new home without knowing it would receive proper care."

"I'll take very good care of your car," she said tartly.

"Oh, I am certain you will want to, but you will pardon me if I reserve judgment until I have spent some time observing for myself."

"And just how long might that observation period take?"

"How long would a man be required to stay to convince you he truly loved you?" The buccaneer dared her, white teeth flashing.

Her heart skipped a beat. For a moment she panicked, realizing he hadn't given up on love, hadn't relinquished his proposal.

What was she waiting for? What would she need to be able to take the next step with this man who had surmounted his own past, his own doubts, enough to believe in her despite the case that Bradley had built against her?

Could she do less? Would she forever deny her heart's dreams, trapped forever in the past, giving up the future that beckoned from this man's eyes?

Suddenly her vision blurred. This man...she could love. This man intrigued her; he didn't scare her. She loved him with all her heart and soul. She wanted nothing more than to wake up to him each morning, lie down with him each night, to share anything and everything in between.

"Fifty years," she said quickly. "With an option for ten more at a time."

He pretended to think about it, brushing one long finger across his chin, a finger she could still see tracing down her body.

Body. Lexie looked down in dismay at her ancient sleep shirt and fear took another stab at her. "Dominic, look at me."

He gave her a slow, thorough perusal, branding his way down her body without ever touching her. "I am looking."

"I can't be your society page partner. I'm not that woman. I'll mix up the forks at fancy dinners. I'd rather die than wear designer clothes." She swallowed hard and held out her arms. "This is me, Dominic—the real me. Holey T-shirts, dirt on my feet."

He stalked her like a lion after his mate, his dark gazing burning her. "The only thing I would change—" His voice turned husky as he stopped in front of her. "Is that you are wearing too damn many clothes."

She stepped back, the look in his eyes stealing her breath. "I'm not a mansion kind of girl, Dominic."

"Fine. We will live here." He kept coming.

"You're not hearing what I'm saying."

"I hear, but you're speaking nonsense. None of that matters." He leaned down as though to kiss her but stopped less than a breath away. "You do not have to believe that love exists, Lexie—the permanent kind. You do not have to believe I will stay. I am prepared to spend every last minute of my life proving both to you, however long it takes."

His body was so close that she could feel the heat from him sinking into her skin. She swayed toward him.

He took a step backward, and she moaned. "I want to believe you. I do."

"I have never let another human being drive my T-bird. No one but you has laid a finger on its engine." His eyes were lasers. "How can you believe I would give any less than everything to the woman who is the very breath of my body? If I would not abandon a heap of metal to another, why would I throw aside your heart, when it is everything to me, every dream I ever had but despaired of finding?"

He closed the gap between them. "You can resist all you want, be afraid as long as you need, but I am not going anywhere, Lexie. Ever."

He traced one long finger down her cheek as he had once traced a smear of grease. "I did not get so wealthy by giving up easily. You will fall in love with me and you will marry me and you will—"

She stopped his demands with her mouth, sealing her lips to his. Gasping an oath, Dominic pulled her into his body so tightly she could barely breathe, his mouth hungry and needy and filled with promises she found herself ready to believe—

Eager to believe. Eager to begin. She dug her fingers into his hair and nestled closer—

Then broke away from the kiss before she lost her mind.

"Lexie—" he growled, reaching for her.

She danced back, just out of his reach. "Aren't you forgetting something?" She managed to smile though her breathing faltered, her heart all but leaping from her chest.

"What? Stop torturing me, you little minx."

She cocked one hip, holding out her hand. "The keys. The deal is not valid until I see those keys in my hot little hand."

His eyes promising delicious retribution, Dominic dug into his jeans' pocket as her eyes followed his hand to see ample evidence of how badly he wanted her.

He tossed her the keys, and she snagged them, closing her fingers around them. He leaned toward her, and she darted around him. "Not now, Dominic. I want to drive my car."

Her legs flew out from beneath her as he swooped her into his arms and turned, heading back toward the dome, his eyes fierce, his grip one she could not break—even if she wanted to.

"Later. You promised that I could try the sultan's bed anytime I wanted. I want it now."

Midnight eyes glowed as his mouth lowered to hers, his lips brushing hers with unmistakable tenderness.

"You drive a hard bargain, Dominic."

"Call me Nikos, Lexie. Please. I want to be that man with you. Always."

Tears of relief, of hope, of a budding new trust blurred her vision. Fiercely, she wrapped her arms around his neck. "All right, Nikos. Seventy-five years. That's my final offer."

His grin could have lit up the world. He shouldered aside the door.

And then Lexie's pirate strode to the sultan's bed as though she were plundered treasure stolen from the sea. He laid her down like something precious and fine, then stood over her, his midnight eyes filled with love and hope and heat and promise.

He held out one hand to shake. "Done."

Lexie slid her hand into his—and then jerked hard.

Nikos lost his balance—

And together they fell into a brand-new world.

* * * * *

ACKNOWLEDGMENTS

My thanks to Phil Sobey—the wizard who restored the models for Dominic's T-bird and Lexie's pickup—for all the car talk. Thanks also to Kathleen Panov for the Easter egg and software advice and to Jonny Brashear for insights into gaming and network security. Monica and Jim Caltabiano taught me about hostile takeovers and poison pills. My appreciation to the folks at Hut's Hamburgers for feeding generations of happy Austinites, including the men of my family. Thanks to Penny Draeger and Vickie Redman for reading the draft and giving me peace of mind during distractions too numerous to mention.

Any errors made or liberties taken are my own.

SILHOUETTE®
MAKES YOU
A STAR!

Feel like a star with Silhouette.

We will fly you and a guest to New York City for an
exciting weekend stay at a glamorous 5-star hotel.
Experience a refreshing day at one of New York's
trendiest spas and have your photo taken by a
professional. Plus, receive $1,000 U.S. spending money!

Flowers...long walks...dinner for two...
how does Silhouette Books
make romance come alive for you?

Send us a script, with 500 words or less, along with visuals (only drawings,
magazine cutouts or photographs or combination thereof). Show us how
Silhouette Makes Your Love Come Alive. Be creative and have fun. No
purchase necessary. All entries must be clearly marked with your name,
address and telephone number. All entries will become property of
Silhouette and are not returnable. **Contest closes September 28, 2001.**

Please send your entry to: **Silhouette Makes You a Star!**

In U.S.A.
P.O. Box 9069
Buffalo, NY, 14269-9069

In Canada
P.O. Box 637
Fort Erie, ON, L2A 5X3

Look for contest details on the next page, by visiting www.eHarlequin.com or
request a copy by sending a self-addressed envelope to the applicable address
above. Contest open to Canadian and U.S. residents who are 18 or over.
Void where prohibited.

Silhouette®

Where love comes alive™

Our lucky winner's photo will appear in a Silhouette ad. Join the fun!

SRMYAS1